YESTERDAY'S

10p

MILLS & BOON LIMITED
ETON HOUSE   18-24 PARADISE ROAD
RICHMOND   SURREY   TW9 1SR

First published in Great Britain 1990
by Mills & Boon Limited

© Kay Gregory 1990

Australian copyright 1990
Philippine copyright 1990
This edition 1990

ISBN 0 263 76894 5

Set in Times Roman 10 on 12 pt.
01-9012-52480 C

Made and printed in Great Britain

IN MEMORY OF CLARA BENSON
'Our Mrs B.'

Whose generosity and warm heart
will not be forgotten

CHAPTER ONE

'SWISS CHARD,' said Anna. 'Can you believe it? She's throwing Swiss chard again this morning, Margie.'

'Hmm?' Margie lowered the financial statement she was studying and peered vaguely at her friend over the top of her glasses. 'What on earth are you talking about, Anna?'

'Swiss chard,' repeated Anna succinctly. 'On the front lawn.'

'Ah.' Margie began to see the light. She sighed, and laid the thick sheaf of papers resignedly on the table beside her chair. 'You mean Mrs Fazackerley. Has she struck again?'

'Mm. In fact she's still striking.'

'Oh, dear.' Margie threw her glasses carelessly beside the all-important statement, uncoiled her long, willowy body and went to stand beside Anna at the window. As she watched, another armful of leaves came flying over the fence to join an untidy heap of vegetation on the lawn.

'It was green onions yesterday,' she remarked gloomily. 'Just the tough green tops of them, of course.'

'Of course. What *are* we going to do about her, Margie?'

'I don't know. I think she *means* well...'

'I'm not so sure she means well at all,' muttered Anna. 'She always plants too much, then when her rows get overgrown she uses us as a handy dumping ground.

Otherwise why doesn't she ask us if we *want* all these mountains of ageing veggies?'

Margie shrugged and pushed a lock of straight blonde hair behind her shoulder. 'Maybe you're right. Meanwhile I guess we're having Swiss chard salad for lunch, are we? Tell you what, you pick it up and I'll run down to the store for some oil and vinegar. We were out of both of them last time I looked.'

'All right,' agreed Anna. 'Salad it is. Again. See you in a minute.'

Yes, salad again, thought Margie as she made her way down the street to Mr Yamamoto's store. Oh, well, things could be much worse, and apart from their eccentric neighbour, really she was very satisfied with her life now that the software company she had founded four years ago was finally on a solid footing. At first the two young women, who had met when they were both students at the university, had only rented the grey and white painted house on Wrenfold Street not far from Beacon Hill Park. But just recently things had been going so well that when Margie was given the opportunity to purchase it she had immediately jumped at the suggestion. Mrs Fazackerley was the only mild fly in the ointment.

When she returned to the house fifteen minutes later, she discovered a huge pile of discarded chard in the dustbin, and Anna at the kitchen sink resignedly washing the remainder.

'You had a visitor while you were out,' she said, turning around so quickly that drops of water splashed all over the white-tiled floor.

Margie noted that her housemate's big round face registered unabashed curiosity.

'Did I? Michael, I suppose.'

As soon as the words were out of her mouth she knew it wouldn't be Michael, the gentle father of five who was her number one assistant at Lamont's Software, and the last person on earth who would be likely to inspire that look of amazed excitement in Anna's wide grey eyes.

'No, not Michael.'

'Who, then?'

'I don't know. He didn't give his name.'

'That's ominous. I thought I'd paid all my bills.'

Anna shook her head. 'This one doesn't look like a bill collector.'

'Oh.' She grinned. 'What does a bill collector look like?'

'*Not* tall and smooth and sexy, with a gorgeous, clipped, educated English voice.'

Margie's face turned a curious shade of grey. 'What?' she whispered. 'What did you say?'

Anna frowned. 'I said he was tall and smooth and—what's the matter, Margie? Don't you feel well?'

'No, I—yes, I feel fine. Did he—did he say what he wanted?'

Anna shook her head. 'He just said he wanted to see you. Margie, what *is* it? You look as if you've seen——'

'I know,' said Margie in a low voice. 'A ghost. Oh, Anna, if he's who I think he is, that's just what he may be. A ghost from long ago...'

Anna's mouth dropped open. 'Oh, Margie,' she murmured. 'Not—you don't really think——'

'I don't know. I just don't know. Is he—is he coming back?'

'No.'

'Oh.' Margie's face turned even greyer as she sank down on to the nearest chair, which gave a loud, sympathetic squeak.

'He doesn't have to,' Anna added quickly. 'He's in the living-room.'

'He's—oh, heavens, why didn't you say so?'

'Nosiness,' admitted Anna. 'I wanted to know who he was.'

Margie stood up again with an odd jerking motion. 'I'd better see him,' she murmured, casting a quick glance downwards at the hot pink shorts she was wearing and fastening the top two buttons of her blouse.

She took a deep breath and walked slowly into the hall.

Eleven years, she thought. Eleven years, and in all that time only that one brief phone call, asking if she wanted to end their marriage. She had said she didn't care, all the while caring terribly, and left the decision up to him. He had said it didn't matter either way, and there the matter had rested. Occasionally she heard from Henriette, her uncle's retired housekeeper who still lived in Montreal, and Henriette said she had seen him once or twice with a woman—women, actually—so Margie supposed his freedom to remarry still wasn't a matter of much importance . . .

Forcing her fine-boned, oval face to assume an expression of cool neutrality, she released the nails that had been digging holes in her palms, hoped fervently that her colour was its normal peaches and cream and, taking another deep breath, opened the door on her past.

'Hello, Justin. How are you?'

She'd done it. Made her voice sound unconcerned and just a little bored.

The man standing easily by the window hadn't changed at all. His smile, which really did quirk up crookedly at one corner, was still disturbingly sensuous—and it brought the memories crashing back. He had smiled like that the first time she had seen him, when even as a little girl of seven she had been struck dumb by an instant and terminal fascination. He had the most seductive lips of anyone she had ever known. Firm, perfectly formed, the lower lip very full and strong. An attractive cleft ran from his straight, flared nose to his mouth and there was a small cleft in his chin too, adding to the strength of his jawline. Deep grey eyes beneath heavy, winged black brows and thick, smooth dark hair that swept back to cover the tops of his ears completed the picture. He was tall, too, powerfully built, and the whole added up to a figure of such improbably heroic proportions that his mere presence in the room had the effect of making her dizzy. As she was now.

She closed her eyes.

When she opened them again she took in that he was wearing a severe dark suit, which only made him look more domineering and untouchable than ever.

'Hello, Marguerite. I'm very well, thank you. And you?'

Her mind went back down the years, hearing the way his clipped voice drawled around the syllables of her name, and suddenly, remembering the hurt, she found she was incredibly angry. Angry that he had come back to disrupt her hard-won serenity. Her blue eyes turned cold, almost as if they had been covered by a thin, hard layer of glass.

'It's Margie these days, Justin. I've been Margie Lamont for years.'

He shook his head. 'No. You don't look like a Margie. Not to me. And why have you changed our name?'

'Lamontagne was never really *our* name, Justin.' She was bitter. 'It was the name we were both born with, of course, and it stayed the same after our—mockery of a marriage. But I hardly think that made it *ours*.'

'Mockery of a...' His voice hardened for a moment, and then he paused and continued evenly, 'I suppose it was a mockery, wasn't it? But I don't see why that was a reason to change *your* name.' The emphasis he placed on the pronoun had a slightly malicious ring to it.

She shrugged. 'I haven't changed it officially. But I wanted a complete break from everything that reminded me of y— of the past. Besides, people out here find Lamont easier to cope with. It's better for business.'

'Business?' He studied the beautiful, closed face before him and she knew he was wondering how it could possibly have anything to do with business. But he didn't voice that arrogantly masculine opinion and only murmured, without changing the cool cadence of his tone, 'You're a businesswoman, then? Henriette said you were working.'

'Henriette? You've seen her?'

'Yes. She gave me your address. Although no doubt our lawyers have it locked away somewhere too.'

'No doubt.' She watched him rest a hip casually on the window-sill and wished her heart would stop thumping. 'Yes, I'm a businesswoman. I own Lamont's Software here in town and I'm happy to say we're doing extremely well. I have twelve people working for me now.'

'Really. I'm impressed.' He didn't sound impressed. He sounded as if he was having enormous difficulty reconciling the cool, capable mask in front of him with the gentle, wistful little sprite she supposed he remembered.

Margie watched the emotion playing across his dark, handsome features, and felt a knot tighten in her stomach. It was a knot made up of anger that he had come back to disrupt her life, fear that she wouldn't be able to handle this situation and, yes, she had to admit it, a return of the old passionate attraction which had held her in its grip, in one form or another, since she had been a seven-year-old fan club of one.

Now she saw that his cool grey eyes were flicking over her with a sort of amused, appreciative surprise. Evidently she was not the vision he had expected. No doubt he remembered a thin wisp of a girl with pale, shining hair the colour of creamed honey. Not the tall, leggy bombshell she was honest enough to know she had become.

She could see that, although Justin was surprised and even a little confused, he wasn't going to admit it. Nor was he enjoying the sensation of not being totally in control of this scene. His hard grey eyes reflected a sort of arrogant superiority, a cool masculine amusement that little Marguerite Lamontagne had become pretty Margie Lamont who was playing at running a business.

'I gather from that superior smirk on your face that you're not impressed at all,' she said curtly. 'Not that it matters. Luckily for me, I don't need your approval any more.'

'Did you ever?' This time the words were a genuine expression of surprise, and they showed Margie, as perhaps nothing else could have done, just how utterly unaware he had always been of her feelings. Well, she wasn't going to give him the satisfaction of explaining herself to him now.

'Not particularly,' she replied offhandedly. 'Why should I?'

'I've no idea. Nor had I any idea that I was smirking, as you put it. In fact I thought I'd given you a particularly charming smile.' He did it again. 'It's good to see you, Marguerite.'

'Margie,' she replied automatically. But as her eyes strayed from his impeccably groomed figure to her own bare legs, bare feet and shorts, she began to see the incongruity of this unlikely reunion which was taking place in her chaotic living-room with its inevitable display of clutter—everything from important financial statements, through odd items of clothing, to boxes which had once contained pizza.

'Won't you have a seat?' she asked formally, waving at the nearest chair.

She was rewarded by another dose of the smile—which was now unmistakably a grin. A crooked and devastatingly attractive grin.

'Where would you suggest I sit?' he asked innocently. 'If there's a chair under that pile of litter, lingerie and literature, I'd say it's a well-kept secret. You haven't changed all that much after all, have you, little Marguerite? Still as untidy as ever.'

His voice had softened perceptibly, and for some reason the way it was drawling around her name again, calling her 'little', made her feel angrier and more disconcerted than ever. But she also had a desperate need to defend herself, to convince him that she really had grown up.

'I may be a bit untidy at home,' she said loftily, 'but I can assure you that I keep my office in immaculate order. Anna says it's an endearing quirk in my character.'

'Endearing? She must be a very good friend.'

'She is,' snapped Margie. And then, seeing the sardonic tilt to his eyebrows, she felt bound to add reluctantly, 'She does clean up after me quite often. When she can't stand it.'

'I'd make you do it yourself.'

Margie glared at him and removed a pile of magazines from a chair. 'The days when you could make me do anything are over, Justin,' she informed him frostily.

'Mm. Maybe they are.' His amused gaze ran lazily over her long, bare legs, and she frowned.

'No maybe about it. And for heaven's sake do sit down. Unless you're planning on leaving.'

'I'm not. And where will you sit?'

'I shan't. I'll stand.'

'Then so shall I.'

Margie shrugged. 'As you wish.'

Again the crooked smile flickered at the corner of his mouth, and she was just about to tell him he could wipe that smug expression off his face or go away when Anna's head appeared around the door.

'I'm just going out,' she told them. 'I have to meet Bill in half an hour, so you'll have the house to yourselves.' She gave them a knowing leer and closed the door ostentatiously behind her.

'What about lunch?' shouted Margie.

'I'll pass,' her friend shouted back.

'Good grief. I do believe she imagines we're about to make passionate love on the sofa,' exclaimed Margie sourly—and entirely without thinking. Then, realising the impression her words might have on Justin, she turned her face to the window so that he couldn't see the flaming fuchsia in her cheeks.

He didn't reply, and when she had eventually cooled down sufficiently to face him she saw that he was looking at her with a very odd expression in his eyes. It was partly amusement, certainly, but there was also something which seemed to be a kind of wry regret. His next words confirmed her opinion.

'The idea is not without its attractions, I agree,' he remarked drily, 'but for the moment it's out of the question.'

'You can say that again,' replied Margie, with more fervour than flattery. Who did this man think he was, telling *her* it was out of the question?

His lips flicked upwards. 'Quite so. Which brings me to the reason for my visit.'

Margie eyed him malevolently. 'You mean you didn't arrive on my doorstep—uninvited—just for the sheer pleasure of my company?'

Justin regarded her with bored disapproval. 'Sarcasm doesn't become you, Marguerite. Especially when it's totally uncalled for.'

Uncalled for? Had he really no idea of the effect he had on her? Had *always* had on her. Didn't he know that the affectionate but casual way he had treated her during the two years of their marriage, and later the equally casual way he had left her, had turned her life upside-down and damaged her heart beyond belief? No, perhaps he didn't, although a man as gloriously handsome and sexy as Justin couldn't possibly be unmindful of his charms. Women must have been falling all over him ever since he'd first learned to walk—with that fluid, animal-like motion that hinted temptingly at a passion and brutal strength which his controlled, sophisticated façade could never quite hide.

Suddenly she felt drained and bone-weary. 'What *did* you come for, Justin?' she asked dully.

He didn't answer at first, then he waved her to her own well-worn armchair as if he owned it and, as she sank into it, said coolly, 'I came to ask you to give me another chance. Or, failing that, an end to this pointless charade. A legal end this time, Marguerite.'

CHAPTER TWO

MARGIE'S mouth felt as though it were filled with acid, and now she was glad that she was sitting down.

'I understand the pointless charade part,' she replied, her voice flat, emotionless, betraying none of her inner turmoil. 'But what do you mean by another chance, Justin? We never had a chance in the first place.'

'Didn't we? Perhaps not. I mean that I'm thirty-nine years old, with a father who's anxious for grandchildren, and a brother who shows no sign of settling down and insists that he'll never get married. I, on the other hand, *am* ready to settle down. It's time. And as you've given no indication that you'd like to marry anyone else, I thought——'

'I see,' she interrupted. 'You thought I'd do.'

She saw Justin's chin jerk upwards and a dangerous light spark from his eyes and, as it had done so often before, her mind went back down the years to those dreamlike weeks after Great-Uncle Charles had died.

There had been just such a light in his eyes then too, when they had gathered in her uncle's study to listen to the reading of the will. Justin, whose branch of the family lived in England, had been summoned across the Atlantic because one of its provisions was that the terms should not be announced until all the beneficiaries were present. These included Margie, Justin, Henriette and the manager of a seamen's charity of which her uncle had been a patron.

When translated from the legal jargon, the will had stated with appalling clarity that the house and the money were to go to 'my great-nephew, Justin Lamontagne'—with bequests to Henriette and the charity—provided that he married 'my great-niece, Marguerite Lamontagne'. There had been more about the joy she had brought to his life since the age of five when, on the death of her parents, she had gone to live with him. Then the clincher. In the event that Justin didn't marry her, the house and enough money to maintain it was to go to her; the rest to the seamen's charity.

Dear, strange, old-fashioned Uncle Charles, who had thought women didn't need much money because there was always a man to take care of them. He had thought he was doing her a favour because he'd known she had fallen head over heels for Justin when she was only seven years old and he had come out to pay them a visit. She had kept his picture by her bed for years.

Thinking back, Margie still winced when she remembered Justin's reaction to that will. They had both been shocked, but he had been horrified. In the beginning she'd thought it would be a toss-up whether he suffered cardiac arrest, swam back to England or jumped off the nearest bridge first.

Instead they had talked about it, both very formal and stilted, and in the end had agreed to get married. Justin because he had been wild with a young man's enthusiasm to start his own branch of the family financial business in Montreal; she because she had been sixteen, in love, and naïvely confident that love would soon grow from their union.

Justin, she remembered, had, like her uncle, assumed he was doing her a favour. Also like their Uncle Charles, he'd thought she wanted to be taken care of and that she would never manage the house on the small amount she would have if they didn't marry.

Glancing up at him now, she saw his grey eyes, very bright and challenging, fixed on her with impatient exasperation.

'No,' he said curtly. 'I did not think you'd "do", as you put it.'

'Any more than you did thirteen years ago?'

'Marguerite, thirteen years ago you were a child of sixteen. I was twenty-six and the thought of marrying a child was *not* my idea of a good time.'

'I noticed. You were hardly ever home.'

'How could you expect me to be? I was busy with the business. It expanded very rapidly, if you remember. Besides...' He hesitated, and a look she would have interpreted as acute discomfort if she hadn't known better passed over his face before he fixed his eyes impassively on two pairs of stockings which trailed in filmy disarray across a chair. 'Besides, we had agreed that, in view of the forced nature of our arrangement, the marriage should be in name only. Surely you didn't expect a dutiful husband?'

'I don't know what I expected,' said Margie shortly, unwilling to admit that she had hoped that being in the same house together would bring them closer.

In fact, although he had been unfailingly kind, and joked with her just as he had when she was seven, their relationship hadn't deepened very much. He had made sure, through Henriette, that all her needs were taken care of, and seemed to assume that, although she had left school to marry him, her life had had all the excitement it needed—talking on the phone, reading, shopping and sometimes visiting friends, occasionally with him, but more often alone or with Henriette. Once he had brought her flowers, and hope had flared briefly, but it had been only his way of showing affection for a child he knew loved gardens.

He had always been good with children, she recollected, remembering how he had entertained her and her playmates when he was seventeen. That was probably what had caused her to fall in love with him then. Later, that childish idolatry had turned to love, because he'd continued to be kind and teasing and tender—when he'd been there.

She shook her head and realised he was staring at her, his heavy brows drawn sharply together. 'I don't know what you expected, either,' he said bluntly. 'To be honest, I don't know why you agreed to marry me at all. At the time I thought it was because you were afraid to make a life for yourself and wanted me to look after you. But that wasn't it, was it? You've obviously done very well on your own.'

'No, that wasn't it,' said Margie, damned if she was going to tell this man who wasn't nearly as kind as she remembered, and who thought she might be a convenient solution to the problem of a grandchild for his father, that she had loved him. Pride had kept her from telling him then, and she certainly wasn't going to surrender her defences now.

'Why, then?' Justin persisted, not letting her off the hook.

She shrugged. 'I don't know. Uncle Charles wanted it—and you wanted the money.'

That startled him. The winged black brows flew upwards and he shoved his hands into his pockets. 'You cared about that?' he demanded. 'Why should you?'

Ah, so she had got to him. She smiled, pleased with his response. 'I didn't need it, and you'd always been nice to me—well, except that once, and even then you didn't mean to be unkind.'

'That once? Oh.' He looked suddenly disconcerted. 'That time when you were a little girl and you ran into the road in front of a car.'

'Yes,' said Margie. 'And you dashed out and snatched me from almost under its wheels—and a very painful little interlude followed. An intimate acquaintance with the flat of your hand applied to a personal part of me that I didn't appreciate at all.'

'I remember,' murmured Justin. 'You ran off screaming that you'd never speak to me again, and you kept that promise faithfully for the remainder of the week I spent with you and Uncle Charles.' He smiled ruefully, his eyes surprisingly tender. 'I felt horribly guilty. I've never believed in hitting children. My father didn't spare the rod and I don't feel that it did me any good. So I thought I must have hurt you much more than I intended, and that I'd made myself your enemy for life. But you scared the hell out of me that day, you know, and I was so angry I lost control for a second.'

Margie laughed lightly. 'I don't think you did me any lasting harm. Anyway, I never ran in front of a car again and the only thing you hurt was my pride. I felt foolish and humiliated—but I understood you did it because you cared about me—then.'

'I still do.' He eyed her sceptically. 'And for that you thought I ought to have Uncle Charles's money?'

'Well…' Margie looked away, not wanting him to read the real truth in her eyes. 'Yes, I suppose so. And as I said, I didn't need it.'

'Mm,' murmured Justin, very thoughtfully. 'So we drifted on like that for two years and then, when I asked you if you wanted to make our marriage a reality—you refused.'

Margie laughed, a high, brittle sort of laugh. 'Yes. You were terribly cool and civilised about the whole thing, weren't you? But after all, we weren't in love, Justin.'

'No,' he said flatly. 'I suppose we weren't.'

'Then you went off to England for five months——'

'And when I came back you had gone.'

'Yes,' she agreed brightly. 'I decided I was old enough to stand on my own feet, so I managed to persuade Henriette that I wasn't likely to fall into the clutches of the Mafia out here—and I've been in Victoria ever since. It's worked out very well. I succeeded in finishing my degree and started my business.'

'No regrets?' His eyes were strangely soft and smoky.

'Of course not. Why should there be? And it left you free to pursue your own life.'

'Hm. Very thoughtful of you.'

His voice, which had always made mincemeat of her emotions, was more clipped and infuriatingly sexy than ever, and Margie, who made a point of never losing control, was hard put to it not to leap to her feet to land a stinging and undeserved blow across his face. But instead, after breathing deeply, she raised her eyebrows and said coolly, 'Why don't you sit down? I don't see how we can carry on this discussion with you looming over me like a—a vulture waiting to polish off the remains.'

'Hm,' said Justin again, his lips quirking. 'And very edible remains at that. You almost make me regret that I'm not a vulture.' But he did as she suggested—dropped on to the sofa after pushing aside several newspapers, stretched an arm along the back of it and crossed his legs. 'Now—where were we?'

'We were reliving old memories, Justin,' she replied sarcastically, her lilting voice gentling over the hard English 'J' of his name as it always had. It was the only sound that had ever betrayed that her first language had not been the same as his.

'So we were.' He ignored the sarcasm this time. 'Tell me, Marguerite, haven't you ever wanted to be free to marry someone else? You must have had a great many opportunities. You're very beautiful...'

Very beautiful. But not beautiful enough for *you*, she thought resentfully. Aloud she only said, 'Perhaps, but I wasn't interested. One marriage was more than enough for me.'

'I see. Is that why you've never contacted me about ending ours?'

'Yes. It hardly seemed worthwhile. And you? You haven't been sufficiently interested either—until now?' Somehow she was managing to keep herself from screaming. She wanted to shout to the four walls that, damn him to hell, she still loved him, although heaven knew why, but no power on earth was going to make her commit herself to a loveless marriage to save him the trouble of looking for someone else.

'Not really. Like a fool, I thought I'd stay young forever.'

She saw his forehead crease, and noticed lines around his eyes that hadn't been there when she had last seen the youthful face of the man she loved.

'It's only been recently,' he went on, 'now that the business almost runs itself, that I've realised time doesn't stand still.'

'In other words, you've got the nesting instinct,' said Margie drily.

'You could put it that way. I'm surprised it hasn't happened to you.'

Oh, it had happened to her all right. For eleven years she had dreamed of the children she never expected to have because she couldn't bear the thought of having them with anyone else. But he would never know that.

'Well,' she replied, 'it hasn't.'

'I see. Does that mean you won't consider my proposition? I had thought it might have advantages for us both.'

Margie eyed him bleakly. 'Just like the last time? No, I won't consider it, Justin.'

He stared at her, controlled frustration evident in every line of his supple body. Obviously he was unused to being thwarted. She thought for a moment, as his long fingers tapped rhythmically against the arm of the sofa, that he was going to argue. But in the end he only shrugged slightly, rose quickly to his feet and said that in that case he supposed there was nothing more to be said. He would put the wheels of a divorce or annulment in motion.

So that was all she was to him now. A wheel to be put in motion so she could be replaced by a more amenable woman—and he was going.

Quite suddenly she couldn't bear it. He was going, and she *had* to say something. As he moved towards the door she sprang up and almost fell across the carpet after him.

'Justin...' She held out her hand and, when he turned around, her fingers brushed against the fabric of his shirt.

His eyes narrowed. 'Yes?'

'Justin, I...'

She didn't know it, but something in the way she was standing, tall, lithe and yet somehow vulnerable, touched him then, and on an impulse he said suddenly, 'Do you want time to think about it, Marguerite?'

Her shoulders drooped. 'No.'

'All right.' He nodded, and it seemed as though he wasn't sure what his next move ought to be. Then she raised her eyes to his, their blue depths big with the tears she refused to shed, and he said, as if the words were wrenched from his throat, 'Have dinner with me tonight, Marguerite. I'm staying at the bed and breakfast next door——'

'You're staying with Mrs Fazackerley!' she gasped, her tears miraculously disappearing at the incredible thought of Justin, who was surely the plush-hotel-with-room-service type, parked next door with the eccentric Mrs F.

'Yes. It seemed the simplest arrangement in the circumstances. Or it would have been if you'd been interested in resuming our marriage.' His face was expressionless. 'However, I'm there now, for tonight anyway, and your clean but peculiar neighbour has categorically refused to feed me anything other than breakfast. So I'd be grateful for your company if you'll come.'

He'd be grateful for... They had been married for thirteen years, and this was the first time he had *ever* said he'd be grateful for her company.

She opened her mouth to say 'no', saw his lips part in that firm, impossibly seductive smile—and said, 'Yes.'

Margie moved the pot of yellow begonias a fraction to the left and then moved them back to the centre of the table. It was the fourth time she had done so in the last ten minutes. She had also rearranged the silver and napkins at least five times and changed her mind about which wine glasses to use at least seven.

Justin was coming to dinner. This unbelievable refrain kept going round and round inside her smooth blonde head. Initially she had accepted his invitation to go out, but almost immediately she had come down with a severe attack of cold feet. The prospect of spending a whole evening alone with Justin, who at last really wanted her for a wife but for all the wrong reasons, was suddenly more than she could cope with, and she had phoned him to suggest that instead of going to a restaurant he should dine at home with her and Anna. She knew Anna's Bill was expected too, and thought she would be able to cope with Justin much better if she was safely protected by the inhibiting presence of her friends.

After a moment's hesitation, Justin had fallen in with the change of plan.

Now, as she rearranged the napkins for the sixth time, she heard the doorbell ring. She glanced at her watch. Seven o'clock on the nose. Justin was as punctual as ever. Then she heard Anna open the door and begin to introduce him to Bill. Oh, lord. She was trapped. Without thinking, she turned to run back up the stairs again like a frightened sparrow fleeing helplessly from a hawk—although she supposed that Justin had now lost interest in the hunt.

When she reached the bedroom her eyes moved automatically to the mirror.

Yes, the soft rose-pink brought out the colour in her cheeks and heightened the blue of her eyes. And the sleeveless cotton dress surely gave just the right impression of uncontrived elegance—so that Justin wouldn't get the idea that she had taken more than the minimum amount of trouble with her appearance. The truth, of course, was that she had changed so many times that Anna had been moved to remark that if she didn't make up her mind quickly, by the time Justin arrived she would have worked her way down to her birthday suit.

'That would certainly get his attention,' she'd added drily, 'which I suppose is the whole idea.'

'Of course it isn't,' Margie had denied hotly, settling on the pink dress and hurrying downstairs to check the table. 'I'm not interested in impressing Justin.'

'Huh,' Anna had grunted, eyeing her friend's departing back with deep scepticism. 'I'd hate to think how long it would take you to get dressed if you *did* want to impress him.'

Margie had ignored her.

As she heard Justin's clipped voice in the hallway now, she gave a last anxious glance at the mirror, straightened her belt and, taking a long, gulping breath, stalked regally down the stairs to meet him.

He was waiting for her at the bottom, with that maddening smile on his lips and his hand outstretched to help her down.

She didn't take it, partly on principle, and partly because she was having trouble controlling her heartbeat and was afraid that if she allowed him to touch her she might lose the power to breathe altogether.

He was dressed casually in dark blue slacks with a grey shirt that almost matched his eyes. He looked expensive, suave and very much in control of the evening, which, Margie was forced to acknowledge, was a great deal more than she was able to say for herself.

'Good evening. You look very cool and charming,' he told her, with a grave inclination of his head.

'Thank you.' Margie had no intention of telling him he looked very cool and sexy, so she led the way into the living-room.

Bill and Anna were standing by the window and Margie was stunned to notice that her housemate's fiancé was helping her on with a jacket.

'Where are you going?' she almost howled at Anna. 'We're going to be eating soon.'

'I know, but I've persuaded Bill to take me out instead,' said Anna blandly. 'You can have the house to yourselves.'

'But we don't want...' began Margie. 'Anna, you can't go out. I've made dinner for four—and the table's set...'

'We can eat the leftovers tomorrow. And it's really quite simple to remove two sets of knives and forks. You could even leave them there if you like.' Anna was smiling smugly and Margie had difficulty conquering an urge to throttle her friend on the spot.

'Anna, please——'

'Don't worry,' Anna interrupted blithely. 'I'm sure you and Justin have loads to talk about.' With an airy wave of her hand, she took Bill by the arm and dragged him out through the door.

Margie glared helplessly after them. When, eventually, she turned her head, she discovered Justin leaning against the wall with his hands in his pockets, watching her with a cynical little smile on his lips.

'Afraid of being alone with me, Marguerite?' he asked silkily. 'I promise I won't attempt to rape you.'

'I didn't think you would,' she snapped at him. 'And no, of course I'm not afraid of being alone with you. We lived in the same house for two years.'

'So we did. To think of the opportunities I missed.'

Margie glanced up at him quickly, and saw that his pewter-coloured eyes were gleaming with an amusement which he wasn't bothering to hide. Why, he was actually teasing her! This man who had stolen her heart and shattered her life so long ago—without even knowing he was doing it—was daring to make a joke out of the fact that he had never attempted to sleep with his own wife. Well—unless you counted that very civilised suggestion at the end, that they might consider conjugal relations.

'Yes, you were a very apathetic Romeo, weren't you?' she taunted, hoping to dent his complacency.

'I thought I told you sarcasm doesn't become you, Marguerite.' His eyes were still gleaming at her, though, as he took a step towards her and asked crisply if he was to be allowed to sit down this evening.

'Of course.' Margie waved indifferently at the grey-and white-checked sofa that was beginning to show signs of wear and tear, and from which she had recently removed all traces of stockings and other clutter. 'Help yourself. Can I get you something to drink?' She walked over to the sideboard and paused with a bottle in her hand.

'Allow me.' Instead of sitting, he took the bottle from her and poured them each a generous gin and tonic. 'To my charming hostess.' His eyes met hers in a long, appraising stare as he raised his glass to her before moving away to lower himself on to the sofa.

Margie followed and took a seat in an armchair which was as far away from him as she could get.

When the silence between them began to be not only uncomfortable but a little ridiculous, she said brightly, 'So—what have you been doing with yourself, Justin, since last we met?'

He took his cue from her and replied with his eyes fixed levelly on her face, 'That question covers a lot of ground. Let's see—I returned to England after I left Montreal, as you know. But perhaps you weren't aware that the reason I was so eager to come to Canada in the first place was that my father and I weren't getting along at all well. He had very strong views on how a family business ought to be run. In other words, the way it had been run since Grandfather Martin moved his family over to England in the twenties.' He smiled, a curving, affectionate smile, and Margie wasn't sure if it was for her or for the memory of a much-loved relative.

'Yes,' she said, trying desperately not to respond to the smile whatever its cause, 'my other great-uncle. I never met him.'

'No, you wouldn't have. Anyway, I was only twenty-four when I joined my father in the business and I was full of what he regarded as new-fangled nonsense about how a financial consultancy should be operated.' The smile, which had been affectionate, turned bleak. 'At the time we were arguing about almost everything, so that when I inherited Uncle Charles's estate I couldn't wait to get away from him to start a Montreal branch of the firm. With enormous relief, I left my younger brother, Marc, to cope with Father and headed with youthful enthusiasm for the New World.'

'Where you made quite a success of the business and acquired yourself a wife you didn't want,' finished Margie with unintended bitterness.

'Marguerite...' He lifted his hand and then let it fall back against his thigh. She saw exasperation flare in his eyes, before he said in a voice that was much more abrupt than before, 'Yes, I made a success of the business. Luckily my French improved with remarkable speed.

And perhaps I shouldn't have married you, but at the time it seemed the only thing to do. I needed the capital Uncle Charles had made from his investments. I thought you wanted protection.'

'And for that you were willing to marry a girl you didn't care for?'

'Marguerite.' Impatience throbbed in every clipped, precisely enunciated word. 'Marguerite, I have always cared for you. I wasn't in love with a child of sixteen, but I saw no reason why the marriage shouldn't work eventually. Our uncle seemed to think you needed looking after, and there are worse things to base a relationship on than mutual need.'

'But I *didn't* need you.'

'No.' His eyes were suddenly hard, probing. 'Then why did you agree to marry me, Marguerite?'

'Margie,' she corrected him promptly. But he was coming too close to the bone. 'We've already been over this. Uncle Charles wanted us to marry and you wanted the money.' She changed the subject quickly. 'If you and Uncle Maurice weren't getting along, what made you go back to England for those five months, Justin?'

He shrugged. 'I was doing well on my own and I thought the time had come to patch things up.'

'Yes,' she said drearily. 'So you left me.'

'My dear Marguerite, you'd already made it quite clear you weren't interested in a normal marriage. Surely you didn't want to come with me?'

Good heavens! The man must have marbles between his ears. Hadn't it been as obvious as snow on a mountaintop that she was crazy about him? No, she had to admit. It probably hadn't, because, knowing he didn't love her, she had done everything in her power to conceal her feelings. And she *had* refused to consummate the marriage. After all, if she couldn't have his love she still had her pride to hang on to. As she had now.

'No,' she said coldly. 'Of course I didn't want to go with you.'

'That's what I thought.' She could hear the relief in his voice. 'In any case, as I said, I decided to patch things up with Father. Which I did. Then I came back to Montreal to find you'd gone.'

'Surely that didn't surprise you?'

'Believe it or not, it did. But I should have known we'd reached a parting of the ways. Funny thing, though . . .'

'What?'

He smiled, an oblique, rueful sort of smile that made her stomach churn. 'I *was* surprised. And I was also a little disappointed.'

Margie clamped a metaphorical lid on the inevitable rush of hope his words inspired and pretended a lack of interest she didn't feel. 'So are you still in touch with your father?' she asked, turning the subject again.

He nodded. 'Oh, yes. He and Marc run the English branch very efficiently; I live in Montreal most of the time, and once or twice a year I leave things in charge of my manager and the family gets together in England. Or, to be precise, in Scotland. I'll be joining them for some fishing next week.'

'How nice,' she said non-committally. 'And Aunt Gillian? How is she?'

'Mother died three years ago.'

'Oh. I'm sorry, Justin. I didn't know.'

'That's all right. You couldn't know, could you?'

'No, I suppose not.'

Margie regarded him covertly and tried to pretend she was studying the lemon in her drink. He looked very lean and handsome relaxing against the grey and whiteness of the sofa. Lean and handsome—and just a bit hungry.

Dinner. She had all but forgotten it. Never mind, luckily it was boeuf bourguignon, which ought to keep. She leaped up hastily.

'I'll just check on the dinner,' she said, flushing for no particular reason. 'Help yourself, if you'd like another drink.'

A few minutes later they sat down, a little formally and stiffly, at the much fussed-over dining-room table—and the begonias were moved for the fifth time because Margie could barely see Justin's face above the blossoms.

'Mm,' he murmured, as she placed a salad in front of him. 'This looks interesting. What is it?'

'Swiss chard,' she replied, poker-faced.

'Really? I believe my current landlady grows it too.'

Margie choked into her wine glass.

'Have I said something particularly amusing?' asked Justin, eyeing her doubtfully.

'No. No, it's not that,' sputtered Margie. She put down the glass, took a deep, controlling breath and proceeded to explain about Mrs Fazackerley and the flying vegetables. By the time she had finished the stiffness between them had gone and Justin's crooked grin was once again causing her heart to misbehave.

To give herself a breathing space from the devastating effect of the grin, she gathered up the salad bowls and hurried out to the kitchen. This dinner was proving an out-and-out disaster. She had intended to keep Justin at arm's length by inviting him into her home, but instead they were being thrown into a highly charged intimacy that left her feeling weak and out of control. Oh, would she have something to say to Anna when her traitorous friend came home.

Meanwhile Justin was waiting for the second course. She took a firm grip on the casserole dish and began to ladle out the boeuf bourguignon.

'This is very good,' he said a short time later, favouring her with an approving smile that caused her stomach to curl. 'You've turned into a very talented young woman, haven't you, Marguerite?'

Margie's temporary good humour was buried under a mudslide of resentment. 'I've turned into Margie, not Marguerite, and I could cook when you were married to me—if you'd ever stayed at home to find out.' She sank her teeth aggressively into a chunk of beef and managed to bite a hole in her tongue.

Justin winced. 'I gather I've stepped on someone's toes.'

No, not my toes, you insensitive bastard, thought Margie indignantly. It's my heart that's causing the problem. 'Don't flatter yourself,' she replied, laying on the acid with a trowel. 'As I think I mentioned earlier, your opinion is of no importance to me any more.'

His hard eyes fastened on her face. ''But it used to be important, Marguerite? Is that what you're saying?'

As she opened her mouth to snap an answer, he held up his hand to stop her. 'And you needn't think I have any intention of calling you Margie. It doesn't suit you. You'll always be Marguerite to me.'

I won't always be anything to you, she thought tiredly. But it didn't matter. If he wanted to call her Marguerite during this one night they were together, then it made very little difference to her.

'Call me what you like,' she said distantly.

He lifted an eyebrow. 'My dear, I can assure you I will. And if you keep up that tone, young lady, I can think of several names I might be tempted to call you— none of them nearly as flattering as Marguerite—which, by the way, means "a pearl".'

'Really? How appropriate, as I seem to be cast before a swine.' Her blue eyes fixed on his with a taunting challenge she knew he would not ignore.

He didn't. His steely gaze raked her in silent specu- lation and came to rest on her face, which was flushed, not only with anger, but with a maddening physical attraction to the raw force of the sensuality he was exuding. There was also more than a little wariness be- cause his grey eyes hinted at swift retribution.

'Would you like to explain that remark?' he asked softly.

'Not particularly,' she replied with a toss of her head.

'I think you'd better.'

Margie looked at the tight set of his jaw, at the white teeth just showing between his lips and the way his hand curled around his wine glass—and she too thought she had better explain. That was no swine sitting opposite her. That was an incredibly sexy man, whose hands she would love to feel upon her body—but not in the way she had a feeling he had in mind at the moment.

'I didn't mean anything,' she said sulkily, and was immediately conscious that she sounded just like the little seven-year-old he had once had occasion to take to task before. 'I mean, it was just something I felt like saying. Perhaps I should have said, "but not a pearl beyond price"—since you've obviously decided I'm not in the least irreplacable.'

'You just don't know when to stop, do you, Marguerite?' Justin's voice was still soft with a certain menace, but she saw that his hand on the glass had relaxed and that he was having trouble controlling a faint quiver at the corner of his mouth.

'I had no intention of starting,' she admitted now, smiling a little.

'All right. Then don't do it again.' He reached across the table to touch a finger lightly to her cheek, and smiled back, a surprisingly gentle smile. Then after a while he asked in an oddly flat voice, '*Did* my opinion used to matter to you, Marguerite? You haven't answered my question.'

She nodded. 'Since you ask, yes. There was a time when it mattered a great deal. A time when I would have enjoyed cooking for you too, if you had wanted me to.'

He frowned, genuinely puzzled. 'But Henriette always did the cooking.'

'I know. She taught me. But since your appearances at meals were so unpredictable, and I was a very new cook, she thought it would be too upsetting for me if I went to a lot of trouble to make dinner for you and then you didn't show up. She said it didn't bother her because she was used to it. Uncle Charles was always just as inconsiderate. It seems to be a Lamontagne tradition.'

Score one for me, she thought smugly.

Justin's frown deepened. 'Inconsiderate? I didn't realise—dammit, Marguerite, it was *my* house, and Henriette was *my* employee. I had every right to turn up or not as I pleased.'

'And you certainly exercised that right, didn't you?'

'Hm.' He eyed her doubtfully. 'I suppose I did. I'm sorry.'

'Save your apologies for Henriette.'

'All right. I will,' he replied, obviously exasperated— with himself or with her she wasn't sure.

'Anyway,' she explained placatingly, 'that's why you never knew I could cook.'

'Mm.' His eyelids, which had been lowered so that she couldn't read his expression, lifted suddenly and he gave her a direct and almost angry stare.

'What else didn't I know about you, Marguerite?' He put down his knife and fork, sat back and waited for her to speak.

She shrugged, not willing to tell him that the one thing about her he had undoubtedly never suspected was that she had been madly in love with him and had, for a few brief, wildly naïve weeks, expected that their marriage would be a real one.

But Justin was still waiting for an answer.

'I imagine you didn't know I could sew and tap-dance either,' she replied lightly. 'I also write very bad poetry on occasions and of course I'm an expert on computer software.'

Justin shook his head. 'So you are. The bad poetry I can accept. But computers! The thought of messy little Marguerite running a successful business—that I still find hard to believe.' He smiled, an unconsciously patronising smile.

'Don't belittle me, Justin. In my own way I'm just as successful as you are.'

'Mm.' He regarded her thoughtfully. 'Yes, of course you are. I didn't intend to belittle you, it's just that it's hard for me to realise you're no longer a little girl. Forgive me?'

The smile was no longer patronising, it was an unabashed demonstration of the Lamontagne charm in action. And he's laying it on by the shovelful, fumed Margie, not wanting to acknowledge that she was already totally disarmed.

'Certainly I forgive you,' she replied primly. 'It's hardly important now, is it?'

'So you keep saying.' He tasted his wine and eyed her steadily over the rim of the glass. 'Tell me what *you've* been doing for the past eleven years, Marguerite. You've heard my story. Now it's my turn to hear yours.'

'Do you mean you actually care?' She was unable to keep the sharpness out of her voice, and Justin's lips tightened with irritation.

'I wouldn't have asked you if I didn't. And I've already told you I care.'

Oh, yes, he had told her he cared. In the way one cared for a young and innocent relation. Only she wasn't so young any more, and he had finally come to that realisation and decided she'd make a suitably biddable wife. Presumably that had been in his mind long ago when he'd suggested she should become his wife in more than name. It couldn't have mattered much to him in those days either, because he hadn't tried to make her change her mind, nor had he attempted to get in touch with her over the years.

But now he said he wanted to know what she'd been doing with her life, and there was no earthly reason not to tell him.

'All right,' she said abruptly. 'Just a minute.' She jumped up from her chair and hurried into the kitchen—ostensibly to fetch dessert, but in reality to calm nerves she had never before suspected she even had. By the time she had taken a number of deep breaths and touched her toes ten times she felt capable of returning with the Grand Marnier parfait.

Then she told Justin, in a quiet, unemotional voice, how she had said goodbye to Henriette and fled to Victoria shortly after he'd returned to England to make his peace with his father. Because he had left an incredibly generous amount of money at her disposal—he had always been generous, she remembered—finances had not been a problem, and after finishing her schooling she had eventually gone on to take a degree in business administration. After that she had worked in the computer field for a few years and then left the company which employed her to work up systems of her own. Eventually, when a few successful sales showed her that she had a very marketable property in her own excellent brain, she had decided to start up a business. Which, she was able to inform Justin with considerable satisfaction, was doing very well, thank you, and expanding.

'I also managed to buy this house,' she finished complacently.

'An impressive list of achievements,' he observed. But he was looking at her as if his mind was not on what she was saying at all, but more on the way she was saying it.

Not knowing how to answer, she cleared away the Grand Marnier parfait, turning down his half-hearted offer of help, dumped the dishes in a disorganised jumble across the kitchen, and suggested they should take their coffee in the living-room.

When she joined him a few minutes later carrying two brimming cups, Justin was already seated on the sofa.

'Come and sit next to me,' he ordered, patting the cushion beside him as Margie headed purposefully for her armchair.

'No, I——'

'Don't argue with me, Marguerite.' As she turned away, he caught her free hand, pulling her down beside him and almost upsetting her coffee.

'Now look what you've done,' she exclaimed grumpily. 'I'm not a child you can order about as you please.'

'I haven't done anything. And I'm very well aware that you're not a child. As a matter of fact,' he continued, casting an appreciative eye over the long legs extending below her pink dress, 'it is just beginning to dawn on me that you're my very own grown-up wife.'

'Not any longer. Never, really,' flashed Margie, edging as far away from him as she could.

Justin smiled, a slow, curving, seductive smile. 'I thought you said you weren't afraid of me.'

'I'm not.' She took a quick gulp of coffee and spilled some on the front of her dress.

Justin pulled a handkerchief from his pocket and held it out to her. As she took it, their hands touched and a current flared between them which for a moment seemed to electrify them both into a strange, waiting immobility.

Then Margie dropped the handkerchief, and Justin picked it up and began to dab without much effect at the coffee-coloured stain on her chest.

'Cold water,' said Margie, in a high, breathless voice. 'That'll take it out.'

'Yes.' Justin put down the handkerchief and, as he moved, his knees brushed against her thigh. He paused and, with his eyes holding her powerless, he stretched out a hand as if some unseen force were pulling it, smoothed the long hair back over her shoulder and curved his fingers gently around her neck.

Margie sat utterly still, transfixed, and then, very slowly, he leaned towards her and the lips, which up until today had never done more than drop a perfunctory kiss on her cheek, moved deliberately over hers—and at long last, now that it was too late, she tasted an instant of that blinding delight that she had been waiting all her life to experience.

CHAPTER THREE

IT ONLY lasted a second. Then, as Justin's hold on Margie's neck tightened and the pressure of his lips became more insistent, the sound of muffled laughter filtered in from outside the front door.

Immediately he released her and lifted his head, just as the key clicked in the lock and Anna and Bill, still giggling, erupted into the hallway.

Margie stared up at Justin, speechless, and saw that the lips which had just parted from hers were no longer gently sensuous, but pulled into a crooked curve. The colour of his skin too had darkened, turning from its normal golden brown to a deep, almost glowing bronze.

'I'm sorry,' he said harshly. 'That was inexcusable.'

With difficulty, Margie found her voice. 'It doesn't matter. In the scheme of things, one kiss more or less makes very little difference.' She forced herself to sound impersonal and just a little bored.

Justin frowned, his face registering a displeasure she hadn't expected. 'One kiss more or... Oh, I see. I suppose you're an expert on kisses as well as computers. I should have known.' He sounded surprisingly bitter.

'I certainly am *not*——' began Margie indignantly. But her vigorous denial was interrupted by the arrival of Anna and Bill, who had apparently brought their amorous scuffle in the hallway to a satisfactory conclusion.

Anna's grey eyes widened as she glanced from Justin's glowering face to Margie's flushed one. 'Oh. Sorry. We're interrupting. Don't let us disturb you.' She grabbed Bill's hand and started to turn away, but in the same instant Margie called after her to wait and Justin sprang to his feet and announced that he was just about to leave.

'Oh, no, you don't have to...'

'Yes, Justin, I think you had better go.'

Anna and Margie both spoke at the same time, and Justin's mouth twisted in a tight, slightly cynical smile.

'Bill?' he queried, turning the smile on Anna's confused fiancé. 'Do *you* have an opinion on this weighty matter? Ought I to stay and make small talk or beat an undignified retreat?'

'Er...' Bill's pleasant monkey-face was split by an embarrassed grin. 'Er...up to you, I guess.'

'In that case it's two to one in favour of my leaving, with one abstention. Marguerite, will you see me to the door?'

It was more of a command than a question, and without being entirely aware of what she was doing, Margie stood up and followed him into the hall.

'Why did you have to do that?' she asked irritably.

'Do what?'

'Make such a production out of going.'

'Did I? I'm sorry.'

He didn't sound particularly sorry, he sounded as ratty and short-tempered as she was. And if this was the aftermath of the Kiss of a Lifetime, she didn't think much of it at all.

Justin paused with his hand on the doorknob. 'Marguerite...'

'Yes?' She raised her eyebrows, trying to look cool and disinterested.

'Marguerite, I have to talk to you again.'

'I'm listening.'

'No, not now. The time and the place are wrong, I think we both need time to—cool down.' He raised a faintly mocking eyebrow. 'Will you come for a walk in the park with me tomorrow? That should be sufficiently neutral ground.'

'Do we need neutral ground?'

'I'm beginning to think so.'

'Mm.' Margie stared at his long fingers gripping the door. 'All right. If you think we have anything to talk about.'

'I have, even if you haven't. I'll see you tomorrow, Marguerite. Is ten o'clock too early?'

'No. It's fine.'

'Good. Goodnight, then...'

For a moment, as he lifted his hand to push open the door, she thought he was going to touch her. But he only brushed his hair back from his forehead, disarranging it, and then stepped quietly out into the starlight. Margie watched his lithe form walk quickly down the driveway and then disappear through Mrs Fazackerley's smartly painted white gate.

With an unconscious little sigh, she closed the door behind him and made her way back to the living-room.

Anna and Bill were now sitting side by side on the sofa, holding hands and gazing mistily into each other's eyes.

'Good grief,' said Margie disgustedly, in no mood at all to appreciate the soulful sentimentality of happy lovers. 'You two look like a couple of moonstruck monkeys.'

'Thanks,' said Bill cheerfully. 'Sickening, isn't it?'

His grin was so infectious that Margie had to return it. 'Sorry,' she apologised. 'I haven't had a good evening, I'm afraid.'

'What happened?' asked Anna, who had no inhibitions about asking personal questions.

'Well, first of all *you* happened,' replied Margie, with a return of her earlier resentment. 'That was a rotten trick you pulled, leaving me alone with Justin.'

'I meant it for the best,' said Anna apologetically. 'I mean, I could see you were still crazy about that incredible hunk——'

'I am *not* crazy about him,' interrupted Margie. 'He's a bastard.'

'I didn't say he wasn't. Bastards can be very attractive.'

'Oh, he's attractive all right,' she agreed bitterly. 'It's just that he wants to play house with me again because he's decided he needs a family, and as I'm married to him already that will save him the trouble of ensnaring some other poor fool.'

'Oh,' cried Anna, aghast. 'I didn't know—you didn't explain... Oh, poor Margie.'

'I am not poor Margie. I'm very lucky Margie because I've managed to escape from Justin's clutches without irreversible damage to my heart. And now I think I'll go to bed.'

'Yes,' said Anna, nodding. 'You do that. I *am* sorry, Margie. I was only trying to help.'

'I know. Don't worry about it.' Suddenly she was too tired to care any more and the thought of upbraiding her friend for leaving her alone with Justin had somehow lost all its appeal. 'Goodnight. See you in the morning.'

She left the lovebirds still gazing at each other on the sofa, and trudged wearily up the stairs to her bed.

As she fidgeted with the pillows, trying to make herself comfortable, Margie noticed that the financial statement which she had started to go over that morning was lying on the table beside her bed. Anna must have put it there,

in a continuation of her long-standing campaign to k
the living-room tidy. Margie sighed. Justin's sudden
appearance had certainly put paid to all her good intentions about getting some work done this weekend. He
hadn't done much for her peace of mind either, she
thought glumly, staring at the glasses which Anna had
placed carefully on top of the statement.

Glasses. She hadn't worn glasses, not even for reading,
when Justin had known her before. Maybe if she put
them on tomorrow it would make her look more businesslike and adult, so that he would stop seeing her as
just a child. But then he *had* stopped seeing her as a
child towards the end of this evening, hadn't he? He had
been in the process of proving that, rather conclusively,
when Bill and Anna had arrived at the inopportune—
no, *opportune*—moment. Anyway, she mumbled to
herself as her eyes began to droop closed, Justin was
neither a book nor a column of figures, and if she wore
her glasses tomorrow his features would only be a blur.
Which would be a waste . . .

At that her eyelids snapped up again. It most definitely would not be a waste. After all, she was only seeing
him again because it had been easier to agree than to
argue. Besides, what could he possibly have to say that
hadn't been said already . . . ?

She shifted restlessly on to her left side, trying to
banish the memory of his kiss. Then, unbidden, came
the thought that in a satisfactorily romantic novel he
would have been so overcome by the taste of her rosebud
lips that he would suddenly have realised he loved her.

Margie laughed into the pillow, a scornful, self-
mocking laugh. Not much chance of that was there? And
anyway, her lips were not rosebuds.

She rolled over again and closed her eyes with determination. No, there wasn't much chance at all—and if she hadn't been such a lovesick fool the idea would never have entered her head in the first place.

This dreary conclusion might have kept her awake all night. But, surprisingly, it didn't.

'Margie, are you at it *again*?' Anna stuck her head round her friend's bedroom door, and gaped at her in amazement.

'Am I at what again?' Margie was defensive.

'Changing clothes. Last time I saw you, you were wearing black trousers and a white top. So what's with the Nile-green jumpsuit?'

'I decided it was too hot for black. Anna, do you think this blue would look better...?'

'No,' said Anna emphatically. 'I don't. Not if that man is due to arrive at ten. It's already five to, in case you hadn't noticed.'

'Oh, lord, is it? In that case he'll be here in...' she glanced at her watch '...four minutes and fifty-three seconds. *That man*, as you call him, is never late.'

'Mm,' murmured Anna thoughtfully. 'On the other hand, it might do him good to be kept waiting. Whet his appetite. Isn't that the standard tactic when you want to keep someone interested?'

'I don't know,' replied Margie, 'but I can assure you that in Justin's case the only thing that would be whetted is his temper. And a very nasty, sarcastic one it can be. He can't tolerate being kept waiting.'

'Hm.' Anna sniffed. 'You do make him sound a charming catch.'

Margie smiled bleakly and dabbed scent sparingly behind her ears. 'He can be charming when it suits him.

But a fish he certainly isn't. What did you have in mind? Bass or flounder?'

'Idiot,' said Anna. Then the doorbell rang, at ten o'clock precisely, and as she went to answer it she threw back over her shoulder, 'Barracuda, I should think. He certainly seems to be ripping you to pieces.'

'I think barracudas operate in shoals,' Margie shouted after her. 'And there's still only one of Justin.'

'You're thinking of piranhas,' Anna shouted back. 'And it's just as well there's only one of your particular fish.'

When she pulled open the door, Justin was standing on the doorstep dressed in grey trousers and a light blue shirt, looking cool and aloof and devastatingly attractive.

Let's hear it for barracudas, thought Anna, at the same time wondering if Margie's sensibilities were in such a fragile state that she would rush up to change yet again when she saw Justin—because blue was supposed to clash with green.

But in that she underestimated her friend, who came sauntering down the stairs a moment later with a composed smile on her lips and a firm hand extended in cautious welcome.

'Good morning, Justin. Won't you come in?'

Justin glanced from Anna to the woman who was still his wife, and when his eyes came to rest on Margie's tall, willowy figure he smiled, a slow, silky smile that caused Margie to turn her head away so that he wouldn't see the effect he was having on her pulse-rate.

But when he spoke, in a low, neutral tone, his reply was cool, and very much to the point.

'No, I don't think I will come in, thank you. If you're ready, we'd better move along before the sun gets too hot.'

Too hot for what? thought Margie involuntarily. And what do you mean, *if* I'm ready? You know quite well you'd probably leave without me if I weren't.

But aloud she only said, 'Yes, of course,' in her best Lady Gwendolyn voice, and after bidding a brief goodbye to a grinning Anna, she sailed past Justin with her nose in the air and preceded him haughtily down the steps.

Behind her, Justin's eyes turned automatically to that part of her which yesterday had been covered by pink shorts. Then there was a flash of red on the other side of the fence as a grey head rose up from the potato bed. Mrs Fazackerley, supervising their departure. Justin grinned and very deliberately stepped forward to place his arm with a proprietorial air around Margie's waist. There was another flash of red, rather more of it this time, and he let his hand drop smoothly over her thigh.

Margie started to push him away, then she too became aware of the interest they were occasioning on the other side of the fence and, rather than create an undignified scene for the entertainment of Mrs Fazackerley, she lifted her chin and pretended the hand wasn't there—even as every fibre in her body screamed at her that it was.

Fifteen minutes later they were strolling beside the stream that ran through the park, and watching the ducks as they bobbed up and down in the water. To Margie's relief—as well as to her chagrin—now that there was no audience to play to, Justin seemed content to keep his hands to himself.

Eventually they came to a sun-dappled patch of grass beneath a willow tree, and Justin gestured at her to sit down.

Margie thought of telling him she would sit where and when she chose, thank you, but there was something so compelling about the way he stood over her, and about the firm pressure of his hand on her elbow, that remaining on her feet and continuing to breathe at the same time became a feat she was no longer up to.

Pulling away from him, she sank down on to the grass.

Justin stared at her, eyes enigmatic, then a moment later he stepped forward to lower himself close beside her. If she moved her fingers just a fraction, they would touch his thigh...

For some time Justin sat with his eyes fixed distantly on the water, saying nothing. Then, as a soft breeze fanned through the willow tree, he said quietly, 'I must apologise to you again, Marguerite. What happened last night—believe me, that was never my intention.'

'Oh, I believe you.' Margie's eyes too were fixed rigidly on the water.

Justin passed a hand across his mouth. 'I don't know why I kissed you. But I promise it won't happen again.' He smiled faintly. 'Unless you want it to.'

He was talking as if she had made some sort of effort to discourage that kiss, which they both knew quite well she hadn't. But, keeping up the charade, she said coolly, 'It's quite all right. And no, I don't want it to. Is *that* all you wanted to talk to me about today?'

'No. It's not.'

'Oh. In that case, if you were thinking of starting on the marriage business again, I'm not interested.'

'I was afraid you wouldn't be.'

Again he fell silent, gazing at the ducks swimming by, and eventually Margie asked curiously. 'Why did you come all this way to see me? Wouldn't it have been easier to phone? I mean, since I was bound to say no any-way——'

'Marguerite, what do you take me for?' He turned to look at her, half irritated, half laughing. 'Surely you don't think I'm that much of an ill-mannered clod? The least I could do was speak to you in person.'

'Yes, I see.' And of course she did see. One thing Justin had never lacked was good manners. She liked that. She would have liked it even better if he'd also had a modicum of sensitivity.

Then, as if he had read her thoughts, Justin added, 'Besides, my dear, I hoped you wouldn't say no.'

'You really thought you just had to snap your fingers and I'd come tumbling into your bed after all these years?' She gaped at him, not quite believing what she'd heard.

'Well, it's a pleasant thought,' he admitted drily, his gaze travelling down from her face to dwell with every evidence of approval on her legs and thighs. A wicked light suddenly lit up his smoky eyes, and as Margie sat stunned, staring at him, he lifted his hand and flicked his fingers in a commanding snap about two inches from the end of her nose.

She swallowed and found she couldn't look away from those glittering eyes. They seemed to be boring into her, holding her in some hot, physical grip.

For a split second they sat there, immobile, and oblivious to their surroundings. Then Margie found her voice and managed to mutter, 'I told you that wouldn't work, Justin.'

'I didn't imagine for a moment that it would.' He relaxed and gave her a warm, surprisingly boyish grin. 'On the other hand the possibilities were—irresistible.'

Margie fought a determined battle with the effect the grin and his eyes were having on her libido—and she won. 'Well, you can forget it,' she told him, in a voice that amazed her by its calm.

He sighed. 'I thought you'd say that.'

He spoke lightly, almost as if he was teasing her. Margie shook her head in exasperation.

'Justin, how could you possibly even think I'd say yes this time? We haven't even spoken to each other for years.'

'I know. That's exactly it. If you'd been seriously involved with anyone else, I'd have heard from you long before now. I was surprised I didn't, to be honest.'

'Mm.' Margie was non-committal. 'I didn't hear from you either, but that didn't cause me to start speculating about your love-life.'

Liar, Margie Lamont, said a voice inside her. You've never done anything else.

'Point taken,' replied Justin. He turned his head back to the ducks.

Margie stared at his profile, taking in the strong jaw, the crooked corner of his mouth and the grey eyes fixed so sternly on the water. She looked for a long time, and then she rose abruptly to her feet.

'If that's all you have to say, Justin, we may as well say goodbye.' She extended her hand to him in a no-nonsense gesture of farewell.

But instead of shaking it, Justin curled his fingers around her palm and pulled her back down beside him.

'Don't go.' Although his eyes gleamed now with a quiet but friendly amusement, there was something in his usually crisp voice that sounded more puzzled than amused. As though he hadn't been sure he meant to ask her to stay and was wondering why he was doing it.

Margie was wondering too. If she knew Justin, the fact that he had travelled all this way only to be rejected would normally have made him tight-lipped and down-right unpleasant. But, instead of brooding, he was turning that twisted, seductive smile on her and saying in a persuasive voice, 'There's something else we have to talk about, Marguerite.'

'What else *can* there be?' She shifted her back against the tree trunk and accidentally touched his shoulder. When she pulled back as if he were a red-hot coal, he grinned at her, this time with very masculine complacency.

Margie scowled, and she was still scowling when she heard Justin say with cool precision, 'I have a suggestion to make to you, Marguerite. Are you interested in getting to know your long-lost family?'

'What?' Margie's scowl deepened with suspicion.

'I said are you interested in getting to know your long-lost family?'

'What family? You mean Uncle Maurice and Marc?'

'The same.'

'Not particularly. Why should I be?'

'I'm not sure. But in any case there's no need to look at me as if I've asked if you want to meet the devil. For goodness' sake, take that revolting expression off your face.'

'What expression?'

He narrowed his eyes and subjected her to a long, appraising scrutiny. 'A thoroughly malevolent expression, I'd say, which I assure you doesn't improve your lovely features.'

Margie glared. 'Are you trying to flirt with me, Justin Lamontagne, as well as talk nonsense?'

'I don't know.' He leaned back against the tree, crossing his arms on his chest and grinning broadly as, with calculated provocation, he brushed his muscular shoulder up her tingling bare arm.

This time, although she drew in her breath, she didn't move her arm.

'I doubt very much that I'm flirting,' he mused, as his grey eyes contemplated the sky. 'I see very little future in it, in the circumstances. On the other hand, I'm not talking nonsense. I'm suggesting that you come to Scotland with me. If not as my newly reconciled wife, then at least to get to know your uncle and cousin.'

CHAPTER FOUR

MARGIE gasped, opened her mouth, closed it again and, without quite realising she was doing it, gripped her hand tightly around Justin's arm.

'Are you crazy? You can't come out here talking marriage, and then, when I turn you down, in the next breath ask me to go to Scotland to meet your family.'

'But I have.' The teasing note was back as he placed his long hand firmly over the small one clasped around his elbow. 'Besides, you've always been shortchanged in the family line, haven't you? It's time we changed that.'

'I had Great-Uncle Charles. And you, for a short time.'

'Yes, and I'm beginning to think I shortchanged you too.'

'You did.' She raised her eyes to his with a sad sincerity.

'I'm sorry for that, Marguerite. I didn't mean to. I was so busy with my own affairs and——' He broke off abruptly. 'It can't have been easy for you—losing your parents so young.'

'No, but they had always been away a lot, on their archaeological digs, so I was more used to Uncle Charles than I was to them.'

'Uncle Charles was an old man.'

'Maybe, but he was glad to have me. With one of his brothers in England, the other dead, and his nephew always abroad, I was really all *he* had left too.'

'Hm,' Justin grunted. 'Even so, it must have been a terrible shock for a five-year-old to be told that her parents were never coming back.'

'Not really. I had a long time to get used to the idea, because they just disappeared, you know. Somewhere in South America, and we never did find out what happened to them. I used to believe they'd turn up again one day, the way they always had before.'

'Do you still dream of that sometimes, little Marguerite?' His voice was very soft now, and the back of his hand rubbed gently down her cheek.

She shook her head, making a supreme effort to ignore the electricity which seemed, almost literally, to spark up wherever his fingers touched. 'No, I'm grown-up now, Justin. And I'm a realist.' She took a deep breath. 'Which is why I want to know what's behind that extraordinary suggestion that I go to Scotland with you.'

'There's nothing behind it. It just occurred to me that you might want to meet your family, that's all. My father and Marc would be delighted.'

She felt a sudden surge of irritation, at Justin, at the effect his touch was having on her senses, and at life in general, which until he had reappeared yesterday had been going exactly as she planned. Abruptly she stood up, tearing her arm from the disturbing fingers which had moved down to circle her wrist.

'You're crazy,' she said for the second time. 'How can I possibly go with you?'

'It's a matter of making a reservation, I believe.'

'Oh!' Margie glared down at his long body sprawled out under the tree and was furious to discover she was admiring it. Did he *have* to look so gorgeous on the outside, when his inside was so very different? It just went to show that you couldn't judge the contents of a parcel by its packaging, even if the packaging was sexy and irresistible and making a curdled porridge of her stomach.

'Are you about to stamp your feet?' he asked, smiling up at her with bland—and infuriating—interest.

'No,' snapped Margie. 'I'm about to step on your face.'

'In that case I shall get up.'

He did so, uncoiling like a long, sexy spring and doing more annoying things to her stomach.

'There. Now *I* have the upper hand,' he said, suiting action to words and placing both his hands firmly on her shoulders. 'Now, stop throwing a very unnecessary tantrum, and listen to what I have to say.'

His fingers were massaging her shoulders. Margie shuddered. 'All right,' she mumbled, feeling suddenly deflated—as well as a little juvenile, because in another moment he would have been right about the tantrum. 'What is it you want to say?'

'I want you to come to Scotland with me. Partly to meet your family, as I said. But also because I think you and I could get along very well together if we tried. I know I'm no saint, but I'm not such a terrible person either. If we get to know each other again you might not find the idea of being married to me so very unappealing.' He smiled crookedly. 'Come with me, Marguerite. I'd like the chance to make you happy, and if you decide you don't hate me—well, that will be something. If, at the end of two weeks you're still adamantly opposed to marriage—to me, at any rate—then I promise not to mention the subject again and we'll end this—mockery, did you call it?—once and for all.'

Hate him? She did sometimes, but that was because she loved him. And she would have found the idea of marriage to him incredibly appealing—if only he had said he loved her.

But he hadn't. Because he didn't.

She turned away from him, tripped over a tree-root and, regaining her balance at once, said tightly over her shoulder, 'Since you're determined to be ridiculous, Justin, I think it's time for us to bring this idiotic discussion to an end.'

She stepped briskly towards the path, but she hadn't taken more than a few paces when she felt his hand once again on her arm, this time not stroking but very firm.

'Marguerite. Wait.' It wasn't a request, it was an order, and as the alternative to obeying would be a very unseemly scuffle in front of two children with a nanny and an extremely dignified gentleman with a cane, she stopped. And immediately wished she hadn't.

Justin's body was pressed up against her spine and she could feel the smooth, hard length of his thigh against her. His closeness left her limp and indecisive, and she found she had lost the will to tell him to let her go.

'What do you want?' she asked in a whisper.

'I want you to think about my suggestion. I think you'd enjoy meeting my father and my brother. You might find you even enjoy *me*. And if that doesn't appeal to you at the moment—you look tired, my dear. I think you could use a holiday.'

'Perhaps, but . . .'

'No buts, Marguerite. I don't have any wish to take advantage of you, or to do anything that might hurt you. I just want to make up for neglecting you in the past. And I want you to be sure before you decide that——' he hesitated '—that we're definitely not suited to each other. I'm neither Torquemada nor Casanova, and I have no nefarious designs on your charming person, if that's what you're thinking. At least, not without your unqualified consent. So think about it, will you? And I'll call round to see you tomorrow. That should give you time to make up your mind.'

His voice had that arrogant, sexy ring to it that drove Margie to contemplate murder—and other things. 'I work tomorrow,' she said crossly.

Behind her she heard a short, exasperated sigh. 'I'll call round *after* work. All right?'

'Yes. Yes, all *right*.'

She couldn't take this for one second longer. Without looking back, she pulled away from him and hurried off down the path.

Anna was out when she got home and Margie was glad of that. All she wanted was time to be by herself, to recover from the devastating effects of Justin's reappearance in her life—and his even more shattering proposal that she should go to Scotland with him—not, she surmised, in order to meet her family, but to give him a further opportunity to persuade her to become his wife in fact as well as in law.

That was the aspect of this whole affair that utterly baffled her. As he said, there would be no legal difficulties about ending their liaison, and as he didn't love her, and she had told him quite unmistakably that she wasn't remotely interested in re-establishing their marriage of inconvenience, why was he going to all this trouble to make her change her mind? She half suspected it was because, once he had decided on a course of action, he didn't like his plans being thwarted. In other words, he liked having his own way.

Pale hair swinging behind her, Margie marched across to the window, spied more flying vegetables erupting over the fence—and decided she just didn't care. They could stay there. Irritably she flung herself down in the nearest chair.

The burning question, of course, was what was she going to do? She did love Justin. She always had and it seemed that she always would. Nothing had changed there. But she didn't think she could bear being married to him if he didn't love her in return. A friendly but distant relationship, interspersed with episodes of physical intimacy for the purpose of producing children—that really wasn't her idea of a marriage. Besides—she wiped a hand quickly over her eyes—it would break her heart.

There were other considerations too, of course. She had a business in Victoria. He had one in Montreal, and she could see no easy solution to that problem either.

On the other hand, if she did spend two weeks in Scotland with Justin, was there a faint chance that he might come to love her after all? He had made no secret of the fact that he found the mature woman she had become far more attractive than the pretty teenager she had been when he last set eyes on her.

Maybe that was it. Maybe this sudden urgency on his part was only a case of galloping lust. Still—he *might* learn to love her...

Don't be a fool, Margie, she admonished herself. You've travelled that road before. Thirteen years ago. And he certainly didn't learn to love you that time. Quite the contrary.

An armful of beetroot tops came sailing past the window and, muttering under her breath, Margie sprung to her feet and went into the kitchen to find a plastic tub. On second thoughts, exercise was just what she needed, and collecting unwanted vegetables was physical activity of a sort...

The following morning she arrived at work late, after a sleepless night tossing and turning, and she spent the day drifting in a mindless fog of indecision that was so unlike her that by three o'clock Michael was suggesting she really ought to go home.

'You're sickening for something,' he told her bluntly. 'After raising five kids I know the symptoms of flu when I see them.'

Maybe he did, but she was willing to bet this was the first time Justin had been explained away as flu. Her strange confusion lifted suddenly, and she smiled.

'If flu comes with dark hair, smoke-grey eyes and a lopsided, curly smile, you're probably right,' she admitted. 'And I think maybe I will go home. Do you mind handling things for me?'

'Of course not. Glad to see you concentrating on a problem that doesn't involve bits and bytes. I gather your "flu" *is* a problem.' He raised his eyebrows. 'By the way, what in hell is a "curly" smile?'

'That's right. Have a good laugh at my expense.' Margie sniffed, pretending to be annoyed with this valued employee who was also a valued friend. Then she smiled again. 'See you tomorrow, Michael.'

Half an hour later she was standing in a white slip in front of her mirror once more trying to make up her mind what to wear. Thank goodness Anna wouldn't be home from the lawyers' office where she worked for at least another hour. Margie could imagine what her housemate would say if she discovered her in the midst of a quick-change act for the third day in a row. Trouble was, this time her doubts made some sense. Justin had said he would 'arrange' dinner, which could mean he was going to show up with a catering service and *coq*

au vin, or a bucket of fried chicken and tired coleslaw—
or it could mean he meant to take her out.

She stared doubtfully at a collection of summer dresses
and finally settled for a neat, sleeveless beige sheath with
a tie belt. If Justin appeared looking tiresomely suave
and magnetic in a dark suit, she could easily run upstairs
and add jewellery which would add a touch of glamour
to the dress.

When Anna arrived home shortly after five, she was
amazed to find Margie seated casually at the kitchen table
totalling up a column of figures.

'Good heavens. No strip-tease today?' she teased.

'No. The old decisive Margie is back,' retorted her
friend with a smile.

'That's a relief. Does that mean you're going to
Scotland?'

'Oh,' said Margie. The smile became noticeably
sheepish. 'As a matter of fact, Anna—I don't know.'

'Decisive, my eye,' snorted Anna. 'Tell you what, I'll
make up your mind for you. *Go.*'

'Do you really think I should?'

'Yes, I do. If you're ready and waiting for him almost
two hours before he's due, I think the barracuda has got
you exactly where he wants you. You'd better go to
Scotland and either get him out of your system—or
marry the wretched man properly. I've watched you over
the years, Margie. I've seen the emptiness in your eyes
when you think no one's looking. Do yourself a favour,
and put that tiresome ghost where he belongs. Wherever
that is. Then perhaps you can get on with your life.'

'Perhaps,' replied Margie without conviction.

Anna noted the unconscious desperation in her friend's
voice and wished she could get her hands on the bar-

racuda. No, her feet, she decided. What he needed was a good swift kick where it would hurt him.

Justin turned up at seven o'clock precisely, wearing a three-piece suit and looking more maddeningly magnetic than ever. Margie, catching sight of him through the window, immediately flew upstairs to put on a choker of British Columbia jade with matching earrings, and Anna, to her seething indignation, was forced to entertain the cause of her friend's confusion.

In the bedroom, Margie was fidgeting with the clasp of the choker when it came to her that she had all the time in the world. Justin had no right to make her feel like a little girl who was keeping her elders and betters waiting. Deliberately she sat down on the edge of the bed. She let a full ten minutes pass before she swayed into the living-room looking as if no man on earth could make her move faster than she chose.

She waited for the anticipated outburst of biting sarcasm. But it didn't come. Instead Justin looked her up and down with an expression of cool appraisal and, apparently approving what he saw, nodded and drawled nonchalantly, 'Very charming.'

'So glad you think so,' replied Margie with equal nonchalance.

Forty-five minutes later they were seated in the window of an intimate little restaurant overlooking the Inner Harbour and Justin was ordering drinks.

'Will you come?'

That was one of the things she had always admired about Justin. He was nothing if not direct, and now that the preliminaries were over he was coming straight to the point.

And she, who prided herself on being equally direct, discovered she had no ready reply. 'Anna says I should.'

'Anna's an intelligent young woman. And that's not an answer.'

'How perceptive of you.'

'Don't be flippant.'

'Why not?'

'Because I don't like it.'

'And what you don't like you don't get?' she enquired sweetly.

'That about covers it,' he replied, not rising even a fraction to the bait. 'What's your answer, Marguerite?'

'I—don't think...' She started to tell him that, no, she didn't think she could possibly go with him. But, as she spoke, his eyes met hers in a look of such awesome intensity that she hesitated. And that was her undoing because she found she couldn't look away, and then she was lost in a smoke-grey void, aware that if she said no to him now, he would go away and she would never have the chance to lose herself in those beloved eyes again.

Anna said she should lay the ghost and, as he said, Anna was an intelligent woman. There was also some old cliché about absence making the heart grow fonder of somebody else. If she said no to Justin, he *would* find somebody else. And that would be the end of hope.

He smiled suddenly, and it wasn't a superior smile now. It wasn't pleading either, but there was something about it that made Margie think for a moment that her answer was important—to him, as well as to her.

She made up her mind.

'I don't think...I can possibly refuse,' she finished in a choking, breathless rush.

Justin nodded, his face once more devoid of expression. 'Good. That's settled, then. I plan to leave on Friday. Will that suit you?'

No, thought Margie in uncharacteristic panic. No, it won't suit me at all. Whatever have I let myself in for? Out loud she only said with hard-won composure, 'Yes, Justin. That will suit me very well. I'm sure Michael can handle the office while I'm away.' That led to another train of thought. 'How long do *you* expect to stay in Scotland?'

'I haven't decided yet. Don't worry, I'll book your flight back for you.'

As if she were a package to be airmailed home when its usefulness was outlived. No, that wasn't fair. He would probably return with her if she changed her mind and agreed to resurrect their marriage. But that wasn't going to happen, was it?

'Thank you,' she said coolly. 'That will be very nice.' When he didn't answer, she added in a low, flat voice, 'But don't be under any illusions, Justin. At the end of two weeks I expect to return to Victoria and my business. You're right that I could use a holiday, and I *would* like to meet your family, but that doesn't mean I'm going to fall in with your dreams about fathering future generations of Lamontagnes.' She swallowed an unwisely large gulp of wine, choked, and put the glass down with a clatter.

Justin waited for her to regain her composure, his eyes glinting with faintly malign amusement. Then he said crisply, 'As you wish, my dear,' and the rest of the meal passed in inconsequential chit-chat about the weather, Montreal, Victoria and, eventually, the details of their Friday departure. He seemed as determined as she was to keep things impersonal, and they succeeded to such an extent that by the end of the evening the atmosphere between them had become positively frosty.

This is ridiculous, thought Margie, as they drank their coffee in silence. He wanted me to go with him to Scotland, I agreed, and now he's freezing me out.

It wasn't until they got up to leave, and Justin's fingers lingered a shade too long on her neck as he helped her with her wrap, that it came to her that *she* was the one who was sending out waves of icy air. She was so filled with doubts about the commitment she had just made to him that she didn't dare let down her guard. And of course he was only reacting to her coldness, taking his cue from her.

A few minutes later he parked his car on the street outside her house and immediately a curtain twitched in Mrs Fazackerley's front window.

Justin smiled thinly. 'I gather my landlady doesn't approve of "goings on" in her respectable neighbourhood,' he murmured into her ear. 'What a pity.'

'There are rarely any "goings on" for her not to approve of, and I expect it's a great disappointment to her,' Margie replied drily. 'Why is it a pity?'

'Oh, I don't know.' Justin gazed blandly at the top of a fir tree growing between the two gardens. 'I just thought it might be.'

'Well, you thought wrong. Why on earth did you decide to stay with her, Justin? She's not your style, even if it is convenient.'

'Just an impulse. I've been doing a lot of things lately that aren't my style,' he replied cryptically.

Such as inviting reluctant wives back to Scotland? she wondered. Funny, she had never thought of Justin as impulsive. Perhaps she didn't know much about him after all.

Without replying, she reached for the handle of the door.

In an instant Justin was out, around to her side and swinging it open for her. Gathering up her bag, Margie stepped out beside him.

When she didn't invite him in he said, 'Goodnight, then, my dear,' and, leaning towards her, kissed her very lightly on the cheek.

She swallowed and stared up at him in silence, and he smiled and said wryly, 'Don't look so horrified. That doesn't count as a kiss.'

'I didn't think it did,' she said stiffly. 'Goodnight, Justin. I'll see you on Friday, if not before.'

'Till Friday.' He lifted his hand in salute and she sensed his eyes watching her as she turned away from him and walked quickly up the path to her door.

Doesn't count, he had said. Well he was right there. That feather-like whisper across her cheek most certainly *didn't* count as a kiss. Oh, no, her idea of a kiss wasn't anything like that at all.

'Marguerite?'

'Mm-hm?' Margie stared down at the sheaf of papers in her lap and tried to look as if she were being interrupted in the middle of important decisions.

The truth was that she hadn't seen a word of the report in front of her from the moment the jet had left Vancouver Airport. The hop from Victoria to Vancouver hadn't been too bad, because it was over as soon as it started and so she hadn't had time to think much about Justin's unnerving proximity. But now they had been airborne for almost two hours and ever since the plane had levelled out she had been conscious of him sitting next to her, his knee occasionally brushing up against hers.

Until today, she hadn't seen him since they'd parted outside her house on Monday night. That hadn't surprised her, because she had learned he had business in Victoria that was not connected with his visit to her, and some of his appointments, apparently, were in the evening. But the moment Anna had waved them goodbye as Justin had pulled his car out from the kerb she'd felt all her nerve-ends start to vibrate. Then there had been the flight to Vancouver, and now here she was, trapped in the air for almost seven more hours, with Justin beside her in his tailored dark grey pin-stripe looking for all the world like a television commercial featuring every woman's favourite dream of the powerful travelling executive. She supposed she fitted right into the picture too, in her severe navy blue jacket and trousers with the neat white blouse, glasses, and her hair pulled back in a tight coil.

'Marguerite,' repeated Justin, this time with a note of authority. 'Are you paying attention?'

'No,' replied Margie, who had been paying minute attention to every slight change in his position ever since they had got off the ground.

Justin reached across and turned the papers she was not looking at face downwards on her lap. 'Now you are.'

Margie twisted in her seat to glare at him. 'Hey, who do you think you are...?' she began indignantly.

'Your husband, for a start. Can't you see me?'

He was smiling at her and there was a look of unusual gentleness in his eyes as he lifted a hand, carefully removed her glasses and placed them inside his breast pocket.

Margie turned her head away and stared fixedly through the window at the sky. 'There's no need to rub that in.'

'There is. It's what I want to talk about. What, in fact, I am *going* to talk about, whether you wish to listen to me or not.'

She sniffed. 'Just because the man next to you happens to be asleep, it doesn't mean you have to start campaigning again, you know.'

'Campaigning?' He sounded puzzled.

'For a convenient, fertile wife who won't cause you any trouble.'

'On that issue, my dear Marguerite, I admit to a temporary defeat. You have already caused me considerable trouble.'

'Good. And it won't be temporary.'

'I usually get what I want in the end.'

'Well, this time you're not going to.'

'Don't count on it.'

Margie was silent, and after a while Justin said levelly, 'You're quite right, of course. I do want to talk about our marriage.'

'What marriage?' she asked rudely. 'To the best of my recollection we never had one.'

'Oh, yes, we did. Remember that little ceremony we attended thirteen years ago? In a church. I think the time has come for us to discuss it.'

'We've already discussed it,' she said tartly. 'But talk if you must.'

'I intend to.' She saw his fingers curl round the arm of his seat and his body tensed beside her before he continued smoothly, 'I've realised, since meeting you again, Marguerite, that I totally misunderstood the situation when I asked you—no, when we *agreed* to get married.'

'We've already been over that, Justin.'

His jaw tightened. 'So we have. But *you* knew I was marrying you for Uncle Charles's money. *I* didn't know that your need wasn't as great as mine. I imagined the bargain we made would be to our mutual advantage. And yet I think you still hold my motives against me. I suppose I can't blame you.'

'I suppose you can't.' Margie stared straight ahead of her, afraid that her face would unwittingly reveal the one thing she didn't want him to know.

'Mm.' As the man next to them let out a thunderous snore, the eyes which she was studiously avoiding lit up with a gleam of pure devilment, and before she could stop him Justin had put his fingers beneath her chin and turned her to face him.

'Marguerite, would you like it better if I told you I married you to quell rumours that I was one of the year's outstandingly successful babysnatchers?' His face was straighter than a poker.

Margie winced and wrenched away from his touch with a stifled gasp. 'Babysnatchers? What are you talking about? And what rumours?'

He gazed at the ceiling and she had a feeling he was searching for inspiration. 'That I was keeping a sixteen-year-old mistress on the side?' he suggested innocently.

'As you'd only been in Montreal a week when we decided to marry, that hardly seems likely,' she retorted.

'Ah, but I was a not inexperienced man of twenty-six. You were only a child of sixteen. Maybe I worked quickly.'

'And maybe you're spinning me one of those tales you used to tell me when I was little. I'm not a child any longer, Justin.'

'I noticed.' His eyes flicked over her, suggesting things that made her flesh tingle. But when she only scowled at him, he grinned maddeningly, ran his finger down her haughtily tilted nose and said softly, 'Yes, I'm spinning you a tale, but you can't fault me for that. You seem to take exception to my honest, if unromantic, excuse for marrying you, and I know what it's like to feel that no one cares. I want to see you laugh again, Marguerite, because I regret very much that I neglected the lonely, confused little girl you must have been.'

What do you mean, you know what it's like? thought Margie. *You* had a mother and father. But out loud she only said lightly, 'It doesn't matter. And you can cut out the blarney, Justin. It's not as effective as it once was.'

It was, though. Ever since he'd come back into her life she'd been desperately resisting the urge to respond to him, to laugh with him as she'd used to do in the past—in spite of the fact that she knew only heartbreak could lie in that direction.

But Justin was raising his eyes as if in supplication. 'You don't have to tell me that,' he murmured. 'I've almost forgotten what you look like when you smile.'

'I don't see why it matters anyway,' muttered Margie. But she gave in and produced a small, self-conscious grin.

'That's better. And it matters because you're a beautiful woman. And I want you for my wife.' It was a statement of fact, spoken with such hard sincerity that she believed him.

Dear lord, if he'd spoken to her in that way years ago, it might have been enough. But it wasn't enough any longer.

'In other words,' she said, struggling to keep her voice even, 'in other words, you need a mother for your as yet unborn children, you happen to be married to me—and it wouldn't displease you too much to take me to bed.'

'If you persist in talking to me in that tone of voice, Marguerite, I can think of another activity that would give me considerable pleasure,' he said severely. 'But if you must put it that way, yes. It would please me very much.'

'Well, it wouldn't please me,' said Margie untruthfully.

'I'm sorry to hear it.' But he sounded more amused than sorry.

'And surprised too, I suppose,' she taunted, turning the papers on her lap the right way up.

'Not entirely,' he replied blandly, turning them over again. 'However, I think the time has come to change the subject. You can tuck your claws in, my dear, and we'll discuss—less *intimate* matters, shall we? I want to get to know you, Marguerite. Tell me all about your computers.' He stretched his long body as far as it would extend in the cramped quarters, and fixed her with a mocking, expectant eye.

Oh, he wanted to get to know her, did he? So he could pin-point her weak spots and work on them to get his own way? She stared at the grey clouds billowing far below her, and shivered for no reason. Still—he wouldn't find any weak spots in her computer knowledge, and it was obvious she wasn't going to get any work done on this plane . . .

Making the best of a bad job, she gave in, and for the remainder of the journey they discussed, quite amicably, everything from computers to finance, family and fishing—and after a while she remembered that one of the very first things she had loved about Justin had been that he was always so easy to talk to...

The only bad moment came near the end of the flight when Margie unwisely asked him what he would be doing after the holiday was over.

'Settling down,' he replied, slanting his eyes provokingly in her direction. 'With you, Mrs Lamontagne.'

'And if that doesn't happen?' asked Margie, her face wooden.

'There are other alternatives.' His voice was suddenly curt, almost businesslike.

Yes, she thought miserably. I'm sure there are—and where in the world does that leave me?

She closed her eyes as pain, cold and black and seemingly inescapable, swept over her in a great dark flood. When the papers she had not been working on slipped to the floor, she didn't even bother to retrieve them.

A short time later, after a calm and uneventful flight, their plane touched down at Prestwick.

CHAPTER FIVE

THE sleek blue car which had been waiting at the airport to meet them swept up the bright, tree-lined avenue towards a large stone building in the distance. As they drew closer, Margie saw that it was much more than just the country hotel she had been expecting, for the carefully tended green lawns, massive entrance and the air of restrained and very old wealth indicated that this impressive mansion must once have belonged to someone of considerable importance.

Margie, who had been to Hawaii and Mexico but never across the Atlantic, made no effort to restrain her gasp of amazed admiration.

'Is *this* where we're staying?' she asked Justin's brother Marc, who was driving.

From the back seat Justin's clipped voice answered for him. 'It is. The Lamontagnes have been staying here for more summers than I can remember. It used to be some Highland nobleman's country seat, I believe. Why? Does it impress you?'

'Yes,' replied Margie with complete candour.

Marc laughed, his dark, boyish face, which was so like and yet so unlike Justin's, lighting up with a friendly warmth. 'I thought the streets of the New World were paved with gold,' he teased her. 'Surely you have your own line in stately homes?'

'I think we have more stately suburbs really,' said Margie, smiling, 'and anything resembling a stately home is usually occupied by someone either prominently political, stuffily symbolic—or in oil.'

'Ah.' Marc nodded. 'Well, in Britain, as often as not, they're occupied by tourists and tour guides these days, or else by an overworked staff attempting to serve your every need. As in this case. But I'm sure you'll find the Glenaron Manor very comfortable.' With a swift turn of the wheel he manoeuvred the car to a stop in front of the entrance.

Immediately Justin was out and holding the door for her. 'I'm glad our accommodations are up to your standards, honey,' he drawled, unsuccessfully trying to adopt a North American twang.

Margie gave him a scathing look and told him he had better stick to finance, because as an actor he would be a national disaster.

'I knew I could count on you to put me in my place,' he murmured, as he helped her out.

'I do my best,' responded Margie, wondering whether Justin could ever be put in any 'place' for long.

Beside her she heard something which was either a snort of reluctant amusement or else a grunt of disgust. A moment later all three of them were standing in a high-ceilinged, panelled hallway as a grey-haired woman in glasses bustled up to find them their rooms.

A few minutes after that she bustled off again, leaving them in Justin's suite as another group of guests arrived at reception. Marc disappeared immediately to his own quarters, and Justin bent to pick up Margie's cases.

Without speaking, he accompanied her up a short flight of red-carpeted stairs and along a long passageway to the door of her room. Just as they reached it a girl with short fair hair, a turned-up nose and a wide, slightly sulky mouth, walked briskly around a corner and stopped dead.

'Justin! I didn't know you'd arrived.' The sulky mouth broke into a bright beam of welcome.

Justin lowered Margie's two cases to the floor and stepped towards her. 'Hello, my dear. How nice to see you again.'

His voice was light, even and affectionate as he took the girl's hands, pulled her towards him and kissed her briefly on the cheek. Her smile became even brighter, and Margie, who was watching the two of them with an irritating tightness in her chest, thought that it seemed a little insincere—or maybe wary.

'How was your journey?' the newcomer asked now, in a cultured, rather high-pitched voice which advertised the worst of all the best schools.

'Very pleasant. Er—my dear, I have someone to introduce to you.' He ran a hand through his hair, leaving it uncharacteristically disshevelled, and turned to Margie. 'Marguerite, this is Catherine. Catherine, this is Marguerite, my—er—my wife.'

Catherine's pale face turned pink, and her eyebrows rose in startled, not altogether pleased surprise. 'How nice,' she murmured. 'Delightful. I—umm—didn't realise you two were together again, Justin. You should have told us.' With another, very social smile, she extended her hand to Margie, and Margie, her own social smile almost a grimace, accepted it and said with forced friendliness,

'It's—delightful to meet you too, Catherine. Although we're not really together again. Are you—er—staying at the Glenaron as well?'

'Oh, yes, indeed. Our families have been staying here together for *years*, haven't they, Justin? Our parents are *very* old friends.' She gave an exaggerated sigh and added with a little pout, 'Only this year I'm all by myself. Mother and Daddy have gone off on a safari—so hot and uncivilised, don't you think? So Uncle Maurice very sweetly asked me to spend the holiday with the Lamontagnes as usual.'

'How nice,' said Margie faintly, echoing Catherine, as she at last found the strength to look at Justin.

He was just standing there with one hand in his pocket, gazing pensively up at the ceiling, and it took all her will-power to resist an impulse to lift her neatly shod foot to give him a sharp navy blue kick in the shins. It was only Catherine's excessively polite and inhibiting presence which stopped her. But she was damned if she was going to stand here one moment longer while Justin gave every appearance of congratulating himself on surmounting an awkward hurdle. Obviously this young woman, who had been staying with his family for *years*, was one of the 'alternatives' he had mentioned—and probably first on the list.

Biting her lip, Margie turned away from both of them, inserted a large key in the lock of room fourteen and tried to push it open. Nothing happened. She tried again. Still nothing. Then, to her incredible irritation, Justin reached over her shoulder—she could feel his cool breath on her neck—and with one quick flick turned it and swung the door inwards. Next he picked up both her cases and placed them side by side in her room.

'Thank you,' said Margie, not looking at him as she stepped quickly across the threshhold.

'My pleasure. I imagine you'll want to settle in now, but I'll call for you again about seven. For dinner.'

Margie was about to say he need never bother calling for her again, thank you, when she remembered that she was twenty-nine years old, too old by far for histrionics, and almost fifty miles from Aberdeen, the nearest large town, alone in the wilds of a country she did not know, very tired, very grumpy, in need of a good night's rest—and quite possibly, by seven o'clock, very hungry.

And if Catherine wanted Justin, she could have him.

'Very well,' she said in a tone that dripped Montreal icicles. 'Seven o'clock, as you say.'

She closed the door on his handsome, faintly amused face with a great deal more force than was required. Then she leaned against it for a moment before gliding across the polished wooden floor to the bed. Sinking on to it, she unpinned her long hair and lay down, staring up at the white plastered ceiling with its intricate design of leaves.

So Justin had invited her to travel across two continents and an ocean because he said she needed a holiday, had never met her family, and because he wanted to make up to her for his past neglect—and possibly, in passing, persuade her to resume what once had been a disastrous marriage.

Manipulative bastard, she fumed. The truth was, he had wanted her to come with him so that she would meet Catherine and, realising there was another fish in the pond, suddenly snap up the bait before that other eager applicant could get it. At least that was the way it looked to her. Otherwise, why had he failed to mention the girl's presence in the hotel before they'd arrived in Scotland?

Manipulative, *arrogant* bastard, she amended, twisting the woven bedspread furiously between her fingers. Did he really think that the fact that some other woman wanted him would make him more of a catch? True, certain women did operate on that principle, but if he assumed she was one of them then for the life of her she couldn't see why he would think *she* was much of a catch. So perhaps that wasn't it at all. Perhaps it just gratified his masculine ego to let her know she had attractive competition.

Irritably Margie turned over on her side. The fact was, of course, that she didn't know what made Justin act the way he did. He really was an extraordinary man, and probably she had never really known him. The one thing she was sure of now was that, whatever devious motives were prompting him, he was a man who was ruthlessly determined to get what he wanted.

Margie closed her eyes, suddenly very tired, and in spite of the fact that it was an unseasonably chilly sun that gleamed in through the window she found she was surprisingly warm. She suspected jet lag, strain and lack of sleep must be the cause of her discomfort. Sighing, she sat up again to take off her navy blue jacket and roll up the sleeves of her blouse.

But, having done that, for some reason she felt even warmer. This was ridiculous. Perhaps what she needed was air. Good, fresh Scottish air. She stood up, walked over to the window and pushed it. It wouldn't move. She gave it an irritable shake, but it seemed to be permanently sealed shut. Shaking her head disgustedly, she went to the door and stepped out into the passageway. Ah, this was better—and there was an open window a few paces down the hall. She hurried towards it and stood there, breathing deeply, grateful for the coolness of the soft breeze and for the green rolling hills of the Highlands stretching before her into a hazy distance.

Then gradually, as she stood basking in cool relief, she became conscious of voices outside. Familiar voices, raised in dispute. And they were coming closer.

A few seconds later they stopped beneath her window.

'Justin, that's all very well, but it wasn't at all thoughtful of you to bring your wife into our midst with no warning.' That was Catherine speaking, her voice even higher than normal.

'She's not the plague.' Justin, *his* voice dry as burnt toast.

'No, of course she isn't, I'm sure she's very charming, but we weren't *expecting* her. We all thought that business had ended years ago, and you *know* your father never approved of your marriage. He's very upset.'

'Father never approved of anything I did. At the time, I expect that was one aspect of things that made the prospect of marrying Marguerite attractive.'

'Really, Justin! Surely you didn't *want* to upset your father!'

'Oh, yes, I did. It gave me great satisfaction. You were probably too young to remember, but we weren't on good terms in those days.'

'I'm aware of that, but after all he *is* your father.'

'And I'm aware of that, my dear Catherine. I have gained a *little* maturity over the years. Father is part of the reason I'm anxious to re-establish my marriage. He'll take a much more positive view of it once he has grandchildren.'

Above them, Margie ground her teeth and dug her nails into the sill.

'Yes, I suppose so. All the same, Justin—well, he *would* prefer an English girl, you know.'

Yes, *you*, for instance, thought Margie savagely.

'Don't you think it's a bit much to ask me to marry to suit *his* preferences?' The words were spoken lightly, but Margie thought she detected the edge of some old bitterness. Anyway he wasn't going to fall for Catherine's line. She smiled grimly.

'Well, yes, I suppose . . .' Catherine's voice trailed off and Margie heard Justin say affectionately,

'Listen, my dear, I appreciate that you're trying to help and I know you're fond of my father——'

'And of you. And—Marc.'

'Of course. And I'm very fond of you too. How could I not be after all the years we've been friends? But please—trust me—I am entirely capable of organising my own life.'

'Well, if *that's* how you feel——'

'It is. But don't be offended. You mean a lot to me, Catherine. You always will.'

There was silence then, and Margie, unable to bear it, pushed the window wide and peered down.

She could just see the tops of their heads, one fair and one dark, and they were standing very close together. Then Justin put his hand beneath Catherine's chin, tilted her face up and touched his lips lightly to her forehead.

'Don't worry, my dear. Everything will turn out all right.' He put his hands on her shoulders, turned her around and gave her a little pat. 'Off you go now. I've got some unpacking to do.'

Margie watched as Catherine went one way and Justin disappeared through a door which she supposed must be directly beneath the window.

She was just turning away when she saw a third figure step out from behind a brick wall that separated the formal garden from the waving green grass beyond. It was Marc, his face very red, and he stopped for a moment, staring after Catherine, and then strode off in the opposite direction with his hands in his pockets and a heavy frown on his youthfully handsome face.

Margie blinked and shook her head, suddenly aware that she had had no business to be listening—or looking—in the first place. Then, very slowly, she made her way back to her room.

A few minutes later she was lying in a cool bath in the old-fashioned, white-tiled bathroom, letting the soothing balm of the water soak into every pore—and the physical aches of the last twenty-four hours began to wash softly away.

The mental aches were another thing, and she wondered for the hundredth time why she had been fool enough to come here at all. She was a bright, intelligent woman, so why had she allowed Justin to talk her into this insane jaunt to the other side of the world? She was a fool, and not only a fool but a first-class, prize-winning idiot.

Yes, she thought, as she smoothed the green soap gently over her body, you may be an idiot, Margie Lamont, but you know quite well why Justin had so little trouble persuading you to come with him. You came because, deep down, and in spite of all the obstacles, you want him to win.

She leaned her head against the back of the bath and ran a sponge abstractedly round her neck. Then she laughed, a hard, mirthless laugh. Oh, sure, she wanted him to win, all right, but even if they managed to solve the problem of their widely divergent business interests it was obvious that the real obstacle to a successful marriage loomed just as large as ever.

It was a very simple, but insurmountable obstacle.

Justin didn't love her.

Her mind returned, inevitably, to the conversation she had just overheard, and her mouth twisted bitterly. So Justin had married her not only for Uncle Charles's fortune but also because it had pleased him to annoy his father. She had been nothing more than a weapon in a family dispute. And now, thirteen years later, he had perceived another use for her. Children. And grand-children for the father he no longer wanted to antagonise.

Margie threw the sponge irritably at the taps, missed, and hit her bottle of shampoo instead. It tumbled off the edge of the bath, but to her enormous relief didn't spill.

Catherine, she thought tiredly. Catherine, who was fond of Justin and from the sound of things wanted to marry him. Catherine, who meant a lot to him too. He had said so. And he had kissed her. Not with passion, it was true, but she would have to be an even bigger fool than she was already not to see that he was at least considering Catherine as possible marriage material.

Without much interest, she wondered where Marc fitted into the picture. Justin had said he wasn't bothered about settling down, but from Margie's vantage-point it had seemed as if he didn't want Marc to settle down either. At least not with Catherine.

The water was no longer cool, it was cold, and she pulled herself out and began to rub a fluffy white towel over her arms and legs. When she was dry she walked into the bedroom and immediately it came over her that, although she had had a few cat-naps on the plane and in the car, she really was incredibly tired.

Without bothering to search for a nightdress, she lay down and pulled up the sheet. Then she remembered that she hadn't set the alarm which was still at the bottom of a suitcase. Never mind. New country, strange bed and a different time-zone. She was bound to be awake before dinner.

Yes, and then what? she asked herself, as she settled the sheet round her shoulders. With Catherine here things were certain to be horribly awkward. She didn't see how she could possibly stay here the full two weeks, and yet...

Then the problem was no longer important, as her eyelids drooped and she fell into an exhausted sleep.

'Marguerite! I said are you ready?' Justin's demanding voice sliced insistently through the door.

'Mm? What?' Margie struggled to open her eyes, saw the evening shadows falling across the window and thought vaguely that she must be dreaming. Where was she, and why was that voice from the past making such an infernal clamour outside her room? She gave a drowsy little grunt, wriggled over on her side and tried to go back to sleep.

'Marguerite? Are you there?'

That much loved but very tiresome voice just wasn't going to go away, was it? She pushed at the sheet, slid her legs over the side and sat up, blinking owlishly.

Oh. Of course. She was in Scotland, and Justin wasn't a dream, he was a very impatient man who was being kept waiting.

'Just a minute,' she called, reaching for a robe which wasn't there.

Damn. Her cases were all locked and just now she couldn't think where she had put her keys. Never mind, the sheet would do for the moment. Peeling it off the bed, she wrapped it around her body and padded groggily across to the door.

'What's the matter?' She opened it a few inches and poked her head out.

Justin, dressed for dinner, was leaning with one hand on the door-frame looking vibrantly alive and as if he was just about to start a long day of high-powered business. He also looked as if he had been just about ready to break the door down.

'It's seven. After seven. I came to fetch you for dinner.'

'Oh. I'm afraid I'm not quite ready.'

'You're not...' Suddenly he took in her appearance, bedraggled, without make-up, but with the sheet held in such a way that it revealed a great deal of warm, pink flesh. The irascible glint in his eyes faded as they narrowed to move slowly over her obviously unclothed figure.

'No. You're not ready, are you? At least...' he hesitated '...not for dinner. That seems singularly apparent.' The words had an edge, and yet there was an amused appreciation in his gaze which he was not taking the trouble to hide.

'I'm sorry...'

'Don't be.' His tone was surprisingly warm now. 'I should have remembered you've had a very long day. Are you at all interested in food now, or would you rather go back to sleep? You can always meet my father in the morning.'

Margie gaped. Justin the mover and shaker, the punctuality freak who never waited a second for anyone, was actually offering to wait for her till morning. Till morning! Oh, no, she couldn't face that. This meal with his father and Marc—and Catherine—was an ordeal she wanted to get over as soon as possible. It would be bad enough in the evening over dinner and wine. At breakfast, over kippers and poached eggs, it would be intolerable.

'No, it's all right. Just wait while I get some clothes on...' She saw his eyes crease at the corners and his lips twitch just a fraction as she went on, with what she hoped was a stony face, 'I'll be right with you.' She started to close the door.

'Oh, no, you don't.' His black leather foot slid smartly into the opening. 'I will be delighted to wait for you, my dear, but I have no intention of cooling my heels in the hall.'

'Yes, but I'm not dressed...'

'I *had* noticed.'

'Yes. So you can't come in, Justin.'

'Of course I can come in. I shall then sit patiently in that large armchair by the window and cultivate a keen interest in the Scottish countryside. I don't see any problem with that, do you?'

Without further ado, and as Margie clutched the sheet frantically against her chest, he put his hands on her shoulders, moved her aside and shut the door sharply behind him.

'There.' He strode purposefully across the room, lowered himself into the armchair and casually crossed his long legs. 'Now, stop glaring at me as if I'm a potential rapist, and get dressed.'

'Justin, you can't——'

'I already have. Besides, I'm your husband. Now hurry up.' He turned his broad shoulders towards the window and, true to his word, began to study the view.

'Of all the arrogant, overbearing...and you're not *really* my husband...'

'Marguerite, my patience is wearing thin. If you don't get a move on I shall begin to take an interest in a different sort of scenery entirely. Rather pink and promising scenery.'

Margie eyed the back of his head malevolently, thought how satisfying it would be to break that large china lampstand over it, then decided he wasn't worth going to gaol for. Resignedly she groped in her bag for her keys, found them, and began to unlock the nearest suitcase.

The first thing she pulled out was the pink dress she had worn when he'd come to dinner. It was relatively unwrinkled and would have to do. Hastily she scrambled into underwear, then the dress, followed by shoes and stockings, all the time keeping a wary eye on Justin's averted head. It was only as she hurried into the bathroom to apply make-up and comb out her tangled hair that it occurred to her that this whole ludicrous scene could have been avoided by the simple expedient of closing the bathroom door. Margie shook her head at the flustered face staring back at her from the mirror. Apparently she was even more tired than she had realised. Her brain must have slipped out of gear.

Five minutes later she told the figure lounging by the window that he could turn around if he liked. When he did, he looked her up and down and, with a small smile on his lips, remarked softly that she was the only woman he knew who could get dressed in ten minutes flat and not look as if she'd just run herself through the fast-spin cycle of the drier.

Her heart gave a traitorous little flutter but, deciding that was the sort of chauvinistic, back-handed compliment she could do without, Margie didn't deign to reply.

A moment later they were in the hallway and Justin, with his hand on her elbow, was guiding her towards the stairs.

'Where are the others?' she asked, as her foot caught in a stair-rod and she almost fell.

Justin pulled her upright, his arm circling briefly and electrifyingly round her waist. 'They're waiting for us in the dining-room. Catherine thought you might want to talk to me alone.'

'Oh. What about?'

'About my disgraceful behaviour in bringing you here without telling my family, I expect.'

Margie glanced sideways, saw the crooked, unrepentant smile and was obliged once again to stifle an urge to hit him.

When she said nothing, Justin asked provocatively, 'Aren't you going to reprimand me, my dear? Catherine says I deserve it.'

'You do. It would have been much easier for everyone if I hadn't been inflicted on them without any warning.' She hesitated, and then added drily, 'Just like the plague.'

Justin shot a quick, glittering look at her face. 'Oh, so you were listening.'

'And watching. But mostly by accident. Is Catherine one of your alternatives, Justin?'

'My what?'

'Alternatives. Remember you said that if I decided not to stay married to you there were other alternatives?'

'Ah. I see.' He stared pensively at a portrait of a long-dead duke who had a very bad-tempered expression. 'I suppose that's a possibility, isn't it? Why? Are you jealous?'

'Certainly not.'

He smiled sardonically. 'I thought you'd say that.'

'Naturally I'd say that. It happens to be true,' she replied frigidly. 'But Catherine's right. You should have warned them.'

'I meant to at first, if you must know. Then it occurred to me that Father had always taken a very disapproving view of our marriage, and I decided he might be more amenable if he didn't have too long to brood. I wanted to make things as easy as possible for you.'

'I've been fighting my own battles for years, Justin. I don't need a knight in shining armour any longer.'

'Don't worry. You won't be getting one.'

They were approaching the door of the dining-room now and Margie lifted her chin, took a deep breath and fixed her eyes rigidly to the front so that when Justin's hand tightened on her elbow she missed the look of exasperated frustration that crossed his face.

Then they were in the dining-room and in a cool, dispassionate voice he was introducing her to the tall, iron-haired man seated between Catherine and Marc at the large round table in the window.

'Good evening, Marguerite. This is an unexpected pleasure.' Justin's father rose slowly to his feet.

Yes, thought Margie. Unexpected and unwanted, that's what you really mean, isn't it? She had understood that at once. The deep voice shook with an undercurrent of anger and the eyes that were grey like Justin's held no welcoming warmth.

'Good evening, Uncle Maurice.' Margie's own soft voice was carefully under control.

As she sank into the chair Justin was holding for her, Maurice Lamontagne sat down, raised his eyebrows and remarked with a scorn he made no attempt to hide, 'I am your first cousin once removed, Marguerite, hardly your uncle.'

Margie experienced a sudden flare of indignation. It was bad enough that Justin was flaunting his second choice under her nose, but on top of that she was *not* putting up with the sneering contempt of his high-and-mighty father.

'I used uncle as a term of respect,' she replied sweetly. 'However, if you don't feel that's warranted, I'll be quite happy to call you plain Maurice.'

Beside her Justin choked into a glass, and on her other side Marc failed to muffle a chuckle. Catherine was regarding her with amazed disapproval mixed with very unwilling admiration. Maurice, on the other hand, appeared to be on the verge of acute apoplexy.

'I think *Cousin* Maurice will do,' he finally managed to bite out at her, through narrowly parted lips.

'Of course.' Margie nodded compliantly, and wished she had managed to curb her irritation. After all, Justin had brought her here to meet his family, and already she had succeeded in antagonising its head. She gave a small, Gallic shrug. The attitudes and opinions of *Cousin* Maurice were the least of her worries at the moment. Besides, she didn't altogether blame him. He probably saw her as a threat to his son's happiness and wanted him to marry his old friend's daughter. A known quantity, instead of some threat from foreign parts. A natural, and commendably paternal reaction.

The soup was placed in front of them, and Catherine, with perfect manners, tried to ease the tension by asking Margie a series of questions about Canada. Her smile was polite and strained, but she still made a very creditable attempt to look interested. Margie was forced to revise her initial impression of Catherine as a spoiled, flighty butterfly. Spoiled she undoubtedly was, but her social sense was altogether admirable. Margie was also forced to acknowledge that she couldn't really fault Justin's taste. Catherine would make a very suitable, sociable wife. Good at children, running a household, and opening garden fêtes.

Marc too made an attempt to help the conversation along, but Justin seemed more interested in observing the efforts of the others, and Maurice, after his initial volley, sat like a stone-faced statue at the table. His mask only cracked once, in a thin smile of satisfaction, when Margie, trying to illustrate the position of Victoria in relation to the Mainland, waved a hand in front of her nose and knocked over a glass of white wine.

The flood was efficiently and effectively mopped up by an attentive staff, but what upset Margie much more than the trouble she had inadvertently caused was the fact that she had given Maurice cause to gloat.

Oh, dear. She had only just met Justin's father, and already she had developed a dislike for the arrogant, rigid old man. So much for blood being thicker than water.

Then the uncomfortable meal was over at last and they migrated to the lounge for coffee. Margie drank hers as quickly as she could and immediately rose to excuse herself on the grounds that she was very tired.

'Justin will see you to your room,' said Catherine firmly.

'Will I? If you say so.' Justin directed a look of faintly puzzled cynicism at the woman he had kissed in the garden, and rose to take Margie by the arm.

As they walked from the room she felt three pairs of eyes pinned with differing degrees of doubt on their backs.

She didn't speak as they climbed the red-carpeted stairs, but outside her room, when Justin released her arm, her eyes came to rest on his impressive chest, and for no apparent reason she remembered her glasses.

'Justin,' she began.

'Yes?'

'My glasses. You still have them.'

'Ah.' His curiously expectant look faded. 'Of course. They're in my room. I'll get them.'

Margie had only just shut the door behind him when he was back, rapping peremptorily on the old dark wood.

'Thank you.' She stood in the doorway and automatically held out her hand; she was a drooping but still deliciously appealing figure in pink.

When her fingers failed to close around the glasses, she looked up.

Justin was staring down at her, an enigmatic gleam in his eyes, and his seductive mouth curled in a way that made her heart bump uncomfortably against her ribs.

She ran her tongue over suddenly dry lips in a motion that was intensely, and quite unconsciously, provocative. 'My—my glasses,' she murmured.

When he continued to stare at her, not moving, she repeated with more assurance, 'My glasses, Justin. You came to give me my glasses.'

'Did I?'

'Well, of course you...' The words died on her lips, because his gaze was now unmistakably sensual, and as their eyes met she knew, with no doubt whatsoever, that the last thing on his mind was her glasses.

Then they weren't on her mind either, as a sensation which only Justin had ever been able to arouse swept over her with an intensity so great that it hurt. And no power on earth could have stopped her now as with an incoherent cry she held out her arms to him in a gesture that was both a demand and a surrender.

CHAPTER SIX

JUSTIN moved with lightning speed, stepping inside the room and kicking the door shut behind him. Then his arms were around Margie's waist, pulling her against him with a violence that would have frightened her if her own primitive hunger had not risen with a violence to equal his.

His hands moved up and down her spine, holding her to him, and she could feel one firm thigh moulded against her leg as his lips came down over hers with a relentless passion that knocked the breath from her body—the body that belonged to him, as it always had and always would—if only there could be an always for them.

But even as she returned his kiss, and their tongues met and twined together, tasting the sweetness of each other's mouths as their hands moved in eager exploration, she knew that this was now, and only now, not the future—and never always.

The knowledge added a desperation to her response, so that as Justin ran his hands roughly down over her hips, she whispered, 'Justin. Justin—please love me.'

Immediately the moving hands stilled, and he lifted his head and held her away from him, his fingers still caressing her shoulders.

'Marguerite—are you sure?' His eyes were grey smoke from a fire which would not easily be extinguished, but even so, she saw the doubt in them—and remembered.

Justin didn't love her. The love he had in mind at the moment was the kind that could be satisfied in bed. The kind that was indistinguishable from lust.

Was that what *she* had meant when she begged him to love her? Perhaps it was, and perhaps this was her one and only chance. If he loved her that way, was it possible the kind of love that mattered would follow? And if it didn't, could she be content with nothing but the memory of a night of passion?

As his thumbs softly stroked her neck, making her almost sick with longing, she knew that she couldn't begin to answer that question until one particular doubt had been laid to rest. This was the wrong time of course, in every way, but how could she even consider giving herself to him yet, when the doubt in her mind was linked to another woman?

'Catherine,' she whispered, her pulses still pounding crazily. 'Justin, was—is Catherine your—girlfriend? You said she was a—a possibility, but—is she in love with you? Have you made promises to her too?'

'What?' Justin, breathing heavily, practically threw her from him. His hair, usually so neat, lay in an alluringly dishevelled sweep across his brow. That, in contrast to the smooth and undisturbed severity of his dark clothing, gave him a powerfully masculine look which was almost threatening as well as quite magnetically sexy. But there was no mistaking the outrage in his eyes. 'What do you take me for, Marguerite? For goodness' sake, woman, I brought you here because I hoped to make you my wife. Properly. For the first time.' His mouth twisted in a bleak, bitter contortion. 'Not to get you into my bed while another woman—one whom you suggest may love me—looks on and lets me break her heart.'

'Justin, I——'

His hands grasped her shoulders again but this time there was no stroking sensuality in his touch. 'And no. Since you ask, to the best of my knowledge, Catherine is not in love with me, I have made no promises to her and she has made none to me.'

'But—you said she was a possibility.' She knew before she opened her mouth that her remark would only inflame him further. But, now that she had begun to destroy all hope that Justin might come to love her, she might as well finish the job.

For a moment she thought he meant to shake her. Then a hard slate shield seemed to come down over his eyes, and he let her go as if she indeed had the plague.

'If we're baring our souls,' he said coldly, 'I suppose there *was* a time when I considered the idea of marrying Catherine. But we never discussed it and I suspect she would have turned me down if we had. As for what I said this afternoon—you'd just finished telling me off, you'd been listening to my private conversation—and you had got very much under my skin, my dear lady wife. As you frequently do. I wanted to see how you'd react.'

'Like a specimen in a lab?' said Margie indignantly.

'Not really. I agree that it wasn't chivalrous, but then you said you didn't want a knight in shining armour.' He gave a short, harsh laugh. 'Have you changed your mind?'

He sounded more weary than bitter now, and she wondered if he had slept at all that day. 'I don't know,' she replied, suddenly conscious of her own tiredness which was rolling over her in great heavy clouds. 'I don't know what I want any more, Justin. But if I've mis-judged you, I'm sorry.'

She raised her eyes to his face and what she saw there confused her. Grim lines still stretched between his mouth and jawline and his features were taut and hard. But behind the hardness she saw something else—something lost and vulnerable. She remembered the very young man who had joked and laughed with her all those years ago, and wondered if perhaps somewhere, beneath the rigid, impenetrable surface, that laughing young man was still there . . .

'I'm sorry too,' he said enigmatically, and started to move towards the door.

Margie knew then that, whatever his intentions had been earlier, he wouldn't try to touch her again tonight. Nor would she repeat her plea that he should love her. It wasn't that she didn't think she could arouse him again. She knew she could. But because of her own doubts and uncertainties she could no longer bring herself to do it.

Justin paused and turned back to her. 'Here are your glasses.' He pulled them out of his breast pocket.

'Thank you,' she said quietly. 'I suppose they'll be wondering what's happened to you downstairs.'

'No. They'll probably think I've followed your example and gone to bed. My *own* bed,' he added grimly.

Their fingers touched and at once they were frozen into a startling immobility. Their eyes locked in a long, naked stare stripped of all pretence and illusion. And in that moment they both knew that, whatever their true feelings about each other, their physical need was so strong now that if Justin did not leave this minute there would be no turning back.

Slowly she took the glasses and her hand fell to her side. It was no good. Her moment had passed and if Justin was ever to be hers, it wouldn't be now. As her eyes dropped from his he extended an arm, almost in slow motion, touched his fingers briefly to her cheek—and was gone.

Margie, drained of all emotion, drained of everything except an incredible, drugged weariness, lay down on the bed without bothering to take off her dress and stared vacantly up at the ceiling. Then faintly from outside she heard what sounded like a muffled curse, followed by a fist crashing against the door-frame.

She pulled in her breath, waiting for further sounds. They didn't come, and gradually the ceiling's whiteness turned black and she was asleep.

She awoke several hours later, saw that it was dark, thought briefly of Justin's lips against hers—and fell asleep again feeling strangely warm and secure.

The second time she woke it was different. She was safe behind the closed blackness of her eyelids but she knew that when she opened them she would have to face the world. A world complicated by Justin.

She remembered the feel of his arms around her and the scent of his body as he held her—and she longed for him to be beside her now. Perhaps he would have been if she hadn't brought up Catherine.

Funny, she believed him now, and she'd been wrong to think Catherine was the problem. The only real problem was herself and the fact that she couldn't accept his offer of a friendly but loveless marriage. It was the best offer she was likely to get, she knew that. Unless she was prepared to settle for a brief affair, of course. But after last night she was almost sure that wasn't for her.

A bird chirped outside and she could sense that the sun was high in the sky. She sighed. However long she tried to put it off, sooner or later she was going to have to climb out of this nice, soft cocoon of a bed.

Very unwillingly, she allowed one eye to admit a slit of light. Then both lids flew open as she realised that not only was the sun well up, but it was very much an afternoon sun. She glanced at the watch she had failed to take off last night and discovered that it was already three o'clock. She had missed breakfast, and lunch as well. That must really have put paid to any hopes she had of improving her credit with Maurice. Not that Maurice's opinion mattered much, she thought resignedly.

But when she wandered downstairs after bathing and pulling on trousers and a red blouse, she found that neither Maurice nor Justin were about. Only Catherine was there, trying to look as if she just happened to be sitting in the hall on an uncomfortably hard mahogany chair. She glanced up as Margie approached, and lowered a book on Scottish flora and fauna. She was holding it upside-down.

'Good afternoon,' she said, smiling politely.

'Hi. Were you waiting for me?'

'Um—well, not—yes, I suppose I *was* waiting,' admitted Catherine, her smile becoming self-conscious. 'Justin and his father have been off fishing together since early morning. I thought they should have some time to themselves, so I didn't go with them, and Marc stayed behind to keep me company. But I've finally persuaded him to play a round of golf.'

'That was thoughtful of you. And thoughtful of Marc to keep you company.'

It was not at all thoughtful of Justin, though, to have left her alone on her first full day in Scotland.

'Marc is *always* very kind,' the other woman agreed.

There was something rather final about that sentence. It went with the funny, closed look on Catherine's face.

'I'm sorry I'm so late,' Margie apologised.

'It doesn't matter a bit. I'm sure you needed the sleep very badly.'

'Lack of sleep doesn't seem to have kept Justin in bed for long,' she observed drily.

'Nothing keeps Justin in bed for long,' replied Catherine. Then she blushed, and giggled. 'Well, I mean . . . oh, dear.'

Margie felt her own face flushing, but it wasn't embarrassment that was making her creamy skin glow. It was the notion that, even if Catherine and Justin had never discussed marriage, that didn't mean they hadn't shared a bed. Then she dismissed the idea as unfounded and unfair—the product of the sort of jealous imagination she despised.

'When do you expect them back?' she asked quickly, changing the subject.

'When they've finished arguing, I expect. They'll have spent the morning concentrating on fish, and the afternoon perched on the riverbank getting on each other's nerves and disagreeing about everything from the size of the fish to Lamontagne's latest contract and the weather.'

'Sounds a delightful way to pass the day,' remarked Margie. 'Why do they even bother?'

Catherine shrugged. 'I think it's the only way they've ever found to communicate with each other.'

Margie looked at her sharply. Perhaps this woman wasn't as frivolous as she seemed.

'What do you mean?'

'Justin was always a self-willed, obstinate boy. Quiet, but determined. A lot like his father, except of course that for years his father had the advantage of age and authority. Then Justin grew up, and things changed. Uncle Maurice hasn't adjusted to that yet.'

'You mean they're engaged in a power struggle.'

'They always have been. I think it's made Justin the way he is.'

'And how is he?' asked Margie curiously.

'Don't you know? I mean, you're—oh, I'm sorry.'

'No,' said Margie, trying not to let her feelings show. 'I don't know. I was very young when we married.'

'Yes, of course.' Catherine's smile was immediate and forced. 'I just meant that Justin's rather—well, impenetrable, you know. Cynical. He always expects that people will try to get the better of him and he hasn't much faith in honest decency and good manners.'

Margie blinked. 'Should he have?'

Catherine nodded vigorously. 'Oh, yes. You have only to look at Marc to see what I mean.'

Margie had looked at Marc, but not with more than passing interest. 'Oh,' she said, 'Um, yes, well, I suppose...'

'You haven't eaten yet, have you?' said Catherine, coming to the rescue. 'Shall I get the kitchen to whip you up a sandwich?'

'Oh, don't bother...'

'No bother.' Catherine was already on her feet and marching purposefully towards the back of the hall.

Feeling a little dazed, Margie sat down on the chair that the other woman had left vacant. She was just thinking that Justin's old friend was a very surprising lady when Catherine was back bearing a crusty brown ham sandwich.

'Would you like to eat it outside?' she suggested. 'The sun hasn't been much in evidence this year, so you might as well enjoy it while you can.'

Margie said that was a good idea, and a few minutes later they were seated on a bench in the garden looking out over well-kept lawns which led down to a field dotted with grazing cows. In the distance the hills loomed soft and hazy, and somewhere a plume of purple smoke billowed up into the clouds.

'It's idyllic,' said Margie, knowing that this moment of loveliness would soon be shattered. 'Now I understand why you and the Lamontagnes come here every summer.'

'Well, as I said, it's not always like this,' admitted Catherine.

'No. Peace never lasts long, does it? Nor does weather.'

Catherine made no reply, and after a while Margie finished the last bite of her sandwich and said quietly, 'Catherine, if I've spoiled your holiday in any way, I'm sorry.'

'Oh, you haven't.'

'You're sure? I mean——' Oh, dear, this wasn't going to be easy, but she had to be certain. 'I mean, you're not in love with Justin, are you? You don't want to marry him?'

Catherine laughed, a high, brittle little laugh. 'Marry Justin? Of course not.' A shadow crossed her face and she added dismissively, 'Well, only as a last resort.'

'Oh,' murmured Margie, deciding not to ask what she meant by that. 'Funny, I had an idea *Cousin* Maurice had you all picked out for his son.'

'He had. Which is another reason Justin won't marry me.'

'I thought you didn't want him to marry you.'

'I don't.'

'No, but—Catherine, I don't understand. Last night I heard you talking to Justin, and he said he'd outgrown the need to flout his father...'

'Maybe he has, but that doesn't mean he'll allow his father to choose his wife. Particularly as he already has one.' Catherine's smile was faintly sarcastic.

Margie tried another tack. 'Why were you waiting for me just now?'

The other girl laughed again. 'Curiosity. I wanted to get to know Justin's mysterious wife.'

'I'm not mysterious.'

'Yes, you are. He's been married to you for thirteen years, yet he never sees you and none of us has ever met you before. *Are* you going to get back together?'

'I doubt it.' Margie stared glumly at the grazing, oblivious cows.

'Mm,' murmured Catherine thoughtfully. 'Life never works out the way one wants it to, does it?'

Margie glanced at her in surprise. So in spite of being the only child of wealthy and doting parents, Catherine had her problems too. But apparently Justin was not one of them.

'No,' she agreed. 'It doesn't.'

They subsided into silence and when Marc came round the corner, whistling, a few minutes later, he took one look at the two mournful countenances staring down at the grass and stopped in his tracks.

'Good lord!' he exclaimed. 'What's this? Have you two just made a pact to give up something nice for Lent? Justin, for instance?' His mouth curled in an uncharacteristic sneer. 'Or is it something more sinister? You haven't by any chance decided that the only solution to your dilemma is to feed him arsenic and hide his remains in the burn? Because I wouldn't altogether blame you. Might do him a lot of good.'

His words were so outrageous, and he looked so puckish standing there with his hands in his pockets and a crooked grin like Justin's on his face, that the terminal gloom fell from both the young women as, smiling, they scrambled to their feet.

'What have you got against Justin?' asked Catherine mildly.

'Nothing.' Marc's reply was brusque and, taking Catherine by the arm, he began to march her towards the hotel.

When Margie glanced up at him, wondering why he sounded almost angry, she saw that he was gazing down at the other woman with a very soft look in his eyes.

Oh, she thought. Is that the way the wind blows? So…maybe Justin was wrong about Marc's disinclination to settle down. In which case she, Margie, would no longer be needed to provide the Lamontagnes with heirs. Catherine could do it.

Instead of bringing her pleasure, this conclusion only made Margie think, illogically, that Marc might have a point about arsenic doing Justin a lot of good.

By the time they reached the hall her temporary good humour had vanished, and when Justin and his father appeared through the door a moment later the first thing their eyes encountered was an exceedingly frosty blue glare.

Maurice Lamontagne returned the glare with one just as frosty, and turned his attention to Catherine. Justin stopped short, raised his eyebrows and remarked with a tight-lipped smile that he hoped her attempt to impersonate Medusa would not prove unduly successful.

'What are you talking about?' she asked suspiciously.

'The likelihood of my being turned to stone. If looks could kill, to coin an original phrase...'

'Oh, don't be ridiculous.' Margie was in no mood for Justin's practised banter, and to add to her frustration he was even more devastatingly attractive than usual. In boots, well-worn cords and a wheat-coloured fisherman's sweater he looked the picture of a handsome country squire. A very windblown, tanned and sexy squire.

'I don't believe I'm being ridiculous,' he replied smoothly. 'But you appear to be in a remarkably bad temper.'

'And you *don't* appear to have caught any fish,' replied Margie childishly.

'We didn't, and I'm delighted to know that our failure is providing you with so much satisfaction,' he answered—with no evidence of delight in his tone.

'*Oh...*' began Margie.

'Quite.' He turned away from her. 'Catherine, have you time for a drink before dinner?'

Catherine hesitated, and then said yes, she had.

Maurice nodded approvingly, Marc watched his brother and Catherine walk away with an enigmatic look in his eyes, and Margie frowned and said she had some things to do in her room.

'Can I get you a drink?' asked Marc, with automatic good manners.

'No. No, thanks, Marc. I'll see you at dinner.'

Without waiting for an answer, she hurried past the two men and ran up the stairs to her room.

Once there, she flung herself down in the chair in which Justin had waited for her yesterday and glared at an innocent picture on the wall.

This insane situation was impossible. Utterly, utterly impossible. She *couldn't* stay here for another two weeks with Justin making love to her one moment and then walking off with Catherine the next. Not, she was forced to add honestly, that she could blame him for choosing Catherine's company over hers this evening. She *had* been in an exceptionally foul mood. She always seemed to be in a bad mood these days.

She ran a finger absently over a grass stain on her sleeve. Well, almost always. Except when Justin touched her or smiled that curving, crooked smile. Then her mood wasn't bad. It was soft with longing. A longing which would only get worse. So now she must make up her mind to stop vacillating and take herself back to Canada—which was where she should have been all along, running her business, shopping with Anna, laughing over Mrs Fazackerley—and not even thinking about the Scottish Highlands—or Justin...

She pulled the first dress to hand from her wardrobe, a white silk with tiny red spots, and as she smoothed it over her hips she decided that, since there was no point in putting things off, she would tell them all at dinner that she was leaving, and ask Justin to make arrangements for the earliest possible return flight.

Shoulders drooping, and feeling as dreary as she had ever felt in her life, Margie threw her two suitcases on to the bed and, with no regard for 'travellers' tips on wrinkle-free packing', began to stuff back the clothes which only a few hours before she had been removing.

When Justin knocked sharply on her door at seven, she was ready.

His eyes flicked over her briefly as she stepped out to join him, and she saw his dark eyebrows fly up in startled approval.

'White suits you,' he murmured, taking her possessively by the arm. 'It makes you look very—virginal.'

'White and red,' Margie corrected him, ignoring the reference to her chastity.

His lips twitched. 'Ah, yes. Red for passion. Perhaps not so virginal after all.'

'Don't you ever think about anything else?' asked Margie crossly.

'Frequently. At the moment I'm thinking about the best way to wipe that semi-permanent scowl off your lovely face. Are you *always* so bad-tempered?'

'I'm not bad-tempered.'

'Prove it.' He stopped at the top of the stairs and swung her round to face him. 'Kiss me, Marguerite.'

'I don't want to.'

'Don't you?' His hands circled her waist and she felt the tips of his long fingers begin to revolve slowly round the base of her spine. He was smiling at her, that lopsided, curly smile that had made Michael laugh at her— was it really only a few short days ago?

'Don't you?' he repeated.

His hand slipped down over her thigh and Margie gave up. She did want to, and she didn't think she could stop herself in any case. Her arms stole around his neck, she raised her lips—and then he was kissing her, and she was kissing him, a long, sweet, gentle kiss that was nothing like the one they had shared last night.

When an elderly couple pushed indignantly past them, they finally broke apart, flushed and breathing a little too quickly. Margie saw that Justin's eyes were very bright and filled with a tenderness she didn't think she had seen in them before. But when she looked again they were only teasing, so it must have been a trick of the light.

'That's much better,' he said. 'Do you realise you're actually smiling?'

Margie promptly stopped smiling, but Justin just laughed and took her hand. 'Come along,' he ordered. 'This won't do at all, I'm afraid. *Not* before dinner.' He grinned. 'Afterwards maybe...'

'There isn't going to be any afterwards,' said Margie, who up until now had quite forgotten her resolve to leave the Glenaron post-haste.

'We'll see,' replied Justin. He wasted no more words, but, still holding her hand, led her sedately down the stairs towards what she was just beginning to think might be her doom. *Would* be her doom if she didn't get away from this man fast. One more kiss like that, one more compelling glance from those smoky eyes, and she could be trapped. Trapped forever in a marriage without love.

Catherine, Marc and Maurice were seated round the table looking subdued, restless and grim respectively.

Oh, lord, thought Margie, this is going to be even worse than last night. But, she added bitterly to herself, no doubt they will all cheer up as soon as I tell them I'm leaving.

She waited until they were seated before saying firmly, in a voice which everyone could hear, 'I've overstayed my welcome, Justin. I'm leaving tomorrow. If you would arrange a flight home for me as soon as possible, I'd be grateful.'

In the silence that followed, Catherine gave a short, stifled gasp, Maurice smiled like a cat who had intercepted a particularly succulent mouse, Marc cleared his throat—and Justin put down his glass very deliberately, turned to her and said, 'Certainly not.'

Margie gaped at him, and all round the table she heard the sound of indrawn breath. 'Wh-what do you mean, certainly not? I want to go home, Justin. I think it will be best for all concerned. And I've already packed.'

'Then unpack.'

'Justin——'

'I think,' Marc interrupted diplomatically, 'that Justin would like you to see more of Scotland before you go. I've suggested to him that perhaps he could take you sightseeing tomorrow. Maybe you could stay for a few more days...'

Margie shook her head dazedly, not understanding why Marc should care. Then she remembered the look she had seen on his face the night before as he'd watched Catherine walk away from Justin in the garden. Of course. Marc thought Justin was a serious contender for Catherine's hand and it was becoming more and more obvious that, even if Marc didn't want to settle down, he certainly wanted Catherine. He probably thought that if Justin's legal wife could keep his brother occupied for a while, he might stand a better chance of snaring his lady.

But she didn't want to go sightseeing with Justin in order to ease the progress of Marc's love-life. She wanted to go home. 'It's very kind of you to think of it,' she told him, as the waitress delivered five substantial plates of Scottish salmon. 'And of you, Justin. But I'm afraid I really must get back.'

'It's not kind of me at all, and you're not going back.'

There was a roughness in his voice which she had never heard there before. It was attractive and at the same time so autocratic that it set all her principles about independent womanhood on edge.

'Justin, you have no right to tell me what to do,' she said, with more conviction than she felt. Sometimes she had a feeling that Justin didn't need a right to do whatever he wanted. And now, suddenly and infuriatingly, he was grinning at her, and his cool grey eyes were gleaming with appreciative warmth.

'Yes, I have,' he said innocently. 'Haven't you forgotten something?'

'What?'

'That you're my wife.'

The air around them crackled with an almost tangible electricity. Catherine's pale face turned pink as Marc's eyes turned to her with deep concern. And Maurice—Maurice was scowling at his son and clenching his fist so hard on the edge of the white, linen-covered table that Margie expected it to snap.

'Justin, Marguerite is absolutely right,' he said, leaning across the table with his jaw thrust out and not giving her a chance to reply. 'She is your wife in name only and she has no business here and she knows it.'

'Father——' began Marc protestingly.

'Uncle Maurice——' murmured Catherine.

'And there's nothing more to be said,' snapped Maurice, ignoring both of them. 'Marguerite really must go.'

'Must she?' Justin was not looking at his father or at Catherine or Marc. His eyes were fixed on Margie, issuing a challenge—and offering her a promise...?

She opened her mouth, meaning to say, 'Yes, I really must go.' Then her confused gaze, trying to escape that disconcerting glitter, fell on Maurice, and she saw the satisfied smirk on his lips and the way he was leaning triumphantly back in his chair—and she turned to Justin and said quietly, 'Maybe I *can* stay for at least one more day.'

Now it was Justin who looked triumphant. Triumphant and altogether self-satisfied. She refused to acknowledge that behind the hard shell of triumph was something else. Something that looked like an overwhelming relief from tension. He leaned back in his chair and raised his glass, once more smiling that cool, complacent smile.

Margie cut carefully into the salmon. She too was suffering from tension, and the smile just made it worse. She glanced at him covertly and he intercepted her look and lifted his dark brows in mocking enquiry.

That was when Margie's renowned self-control flew out the window. Without pausing to think, she lifted her left foot and dug the heel of her shoe smartly into his ankle.

A shadow of pain crossed his face but he gave no other indication that he had felt anything—not until a few minutes later when she heard him murmur, 'Bitch,' under his breath as a heavy foot descended on her toes.

'Ouch,' cried Margie, and then was furious because she hadn't managed to be as stoical as Justin. Several nearby diners shifted in their chairs and she saw three pairs of eyes at her own table stare at her in surprise— and one pair gaze blandly up at the clouds. 'Oh, excuse me, I—I hit my knee on the table,' she muttered ridiculously.

Three heads nodded doubtfully. One continued to study the view from the window with total absorption.

By the time they reached the lounge for coffee, Margie had worked herself up to a fever of indignation. Had she really said she would go sightseeing with this man tomorrow? Yes, she had, and it was the stupidest promise she'd ever made.

It wasn't until much later, during coffee and more awkward conversation, that Margie finally began to stop plotting inventive revenges. By that time she was beginning to realise that Justin's counter-attack had not been unjustified. And the honours, as usual, had definitely gone to him. Her lips twitched, their eyes met, and in a moment she found herself laughing. Justin joined in while the other three sipped their coffee and looked bewildered. Maurice looked thoroughly disgusted as well.

So much for August resolutions, thought Margie, as she tumbled into bed much later feeling almost light-headed. She had set out to tell Justin she was going home, and now she was going out with him instead. It made no sense. Nothing made sense. With a sigh, and a shrug of resignation, she decided she might as well give up for now and let the future take care of itself.

It would anyway.

When, next morning, she awoke to the sound of persistent rain drizzling on to the window, she thought at first that any brief future she might have had with Justin had been neatly outmanoeuvred by the weather. But she reckoned without Justin's arrogant conviction that if he had made a particular plan for the day then naturally it had to be carried out.

At breakfast, dressed in jeans and a warm blue sweatshirt, she remarked tentatively that as the weather was obviously against them perhaps she ought to stick to her original idea and return to Victoria at once.

'Nonsense.' Justin dismissed her comment as unworthy of consideration. 'If we allowed the weather to influence what we did up here, we'd never move out of the hotel, and personally I have no intention of spending my holidays lounging in the Glenaron bar drinking the local malt—excellent though it is—and gazing at heavy

Victorian prints of stags with improbably splendid antlers.'

'Which describes the Glenaron bar to a "T",' nodded Marc, with a grin. 'Justin's right, Marguerite. You can't let the rain stop you up here.'

No, thought Margie, particularly as our departure will leave you free to spend the day with Catherine. She wondered idly what they would do about Maurice and then decided it wasn't her problem.

Shortly afterwards, in a cold and blowing rain, Justin and Margie loaded the car with blankets, along with sandwiches and tea provided by the hotel, and drove off—not into the sunset, but into a stunningly impressive example of a Highland summer storm.

As they crested a hill the wind whipped around the car, bending the few sparse trees at the roadside almost double, and Margie, narrowing her eyes, found that she could only see a few feet ahead.

'Shouldn't we go back?' she asked doubtfully.

'What for?' Justin laughed, and seemed to be enjoying the battle to keep the car on the road.

'Because we can't see anything anyway.'

'It'll pass. Is there anything special you want to see?'

'Something dry,' suggested Margie.

'I could do you a nice tour of the local whisky distillery,' said Justin, grinning. 'That should warm you up. Or how about a genuine Scottish castle? Craigievar, Fyvie, Brodie——'

'I don't need warming up,' she interrupted.

'Don't you?' His eyes glinted sideways, running swiftly over her body. Then he turned back to concentrate on the road, leaving Margie feeling suddenly much too hot. No, she certainly *didn't* need warming up.

'I'd like to see a castle,' she said quickly. 'The nearest one.'

'Probably Craigievar. All right, your wish is my command.' He swung the wheel sharply, and soon they were doubling back the way they had come and half an hour later they were driving past green fields and then pulling to a stop in a car park at the top of a rainswept hill. After that they were running hand in hand through the downpour towards a high, pink-walled tower which seemed to rise up out of the landscape as though it were part of the hillside, put there by nature or magic, but not by the hand of man.

Margie had only time for a quick glimpse of the outside of this jewel of a traditional Scottish tower-house which had once been the seat of the Forbes family, before the cone-shaped, fairy-tale turrets and rounded cupolas had vanished and Justin was pulling her through the entrance and into the dryness inside.

In the small, paved vestibule they leaned against each other, laughing, until their eyes met and they sprang hastily and self-consciously apart. When they walked up the straight granite stairway to the first floor, there was a wide space between them which they were both very careful to maintain.

Margie was genuinely fascinated by the beauty of the baronial hall with its plaid furnishings and soaring vaulted ceiling and, as they climbed higher, by the much simpler Tartan Bedroom and rooms above. But all the time, as she exclaimed over friezes and pictures and carved oak panelling, she was aware of Justin, close to her but never touching. Once she even felt his spice-warm, intoxicating breath on her cheek. And in spite of her enjoyment of the surroundings and his company, she was sad, as if something wonderful was about to be taken away from her. Something wonderful which perhaps she had never quite had.

Then the rain made a last rattling assault on the windows and suddenly stopped. Margie's mood lightened as the clouds rolled back and the square tower where they were standing was bathed in golden sunshine. In front of them for miles stretched the Highland country-side, washed bright emerald in the light.

Later, as they emerged into the garden after exploring every inch of the six floors of the castle, Margie looked up at Justin and smiled. 'That was lovely,' she told him softly.

'Yes,' said Justin. 'Lovely indeed.' He wasn't looking at Craigievar but at the glowing face of the wide-eyed woman beside him. Then he turned away from her and said harshly, 'Did you notice Red Sir John's motto, Marguerite? "Do not vaiken sleiping dogs".'

Something in the bleakness of his voice told Margie that he was not talking about any seventeenth-century baronet, but about a very vital, virile and modern man whom she would never have thought of likening to a dog, sleeping or otherwise. Glancing up now at the hard angles of his face, she wondered what she had said to make him angry.

They returned to the car in silence, and Justin drove off still with that hard look on his face.

All right, thought Margie. All right. She hadn't asked him to show her the country. If he wanted to behave like some brooding Gothic hero, who was she to stop him? He could brood all he liked.

Somewhere around lunchtime Justin pulled the car to a halt above a steep, deserted riverbank. On the other side of the winding mountain road, purple hills carpeted in heather rose up to catch at the grey-tinged clouds above. Below them, a shallow, turbulent river rushed over the rocks on its journey to meet a much larger river and the sea.

Justin pulled blankets and the sandwiches from the car and, taking Margie tightly by the arm, helped her down the slippery banks to a secluded grove of trees near the water. Then he spread the blankets on a patch of sturdy grass surrounded by rocks and boulders and, still saying nothing, waved at her to sit down.

She did, pulling her warm navy jacket protectively around her shoulders. After a moment's hesitation Justin too sank down—as far away from her as he could get without moving off the blankets. Then he solemnly handed her a sandwich.

Heavens, he *was* having a nice brood, wasn't he? Margie contemplated doing something to disrupt it and then decided not to.

The silence continued unbroken for several minutes as the water tumbled over the rocks and the breeze made a lonely sound through the trees. With no conversation to distract them, the sandwiches, washed down by tea, disappeared with remarkable speed. Then Justin gathered up the wrappings, stuffed them into a brown bag and, still without saying anything, lay back on the blankets with his hands loosely clasped behind his head. Only then did he really look at her, from the relatively safe distance of the ground.

Margie returned his scrutiny, smiling slightly, and liking the way he looked, strong and yet relaxed in his fisherman's sweater with the snug brown cords clinging firmly around his hips. All the same, she was damned if she was going to be the first to break this incomprehensible silence.

In the end Justin returned her smile and said quietly, 'This wasn't a good idea, was it?'

'What do you mean?'

'Us. Alone. In this wild and lonely country. We're probably the only people who have come this way for years.'

'I—why wasn't it a good idea, Justin?'

His mouth curved wryly. 'Because I want you. I think you also want me, but I have a feeling that if I so much as touched you now you'd flee like Cinderella on the stroke of midnight—and I'd be left without even a slipper to bring you back.'

So that was the cause of his brooding. He wanted her, but was afraid to make a false move in case he scared her away.

'*Do* you want me, Marguerite?' His voice was suddenly hard, the voice of authority, permitting no evasion or deceit.

And there was no point in denying it. Her eyes ran wistfully over the lean body stretched out so temptingly beside her. 'Yes,' she admitted slowly. 'Yes, I do want you, Justin. But I don't intend to have you.'

'Why not?'

'Because—because wanting isn't enough.'

'I see.' His eyes were as bleak as rain on the moors and just for a moment Margie thought he was in pain. She was about to reach out to him, wanting to smooth the deep lines across his brow, when he added unpleasantly, 'In that case, perhaps I should concentrate my attentions on Catherine.'

Margie gasped, knowing he had meant to hurt her. 'Catherine is in love with Marc, Justin,' she said quietly.

'What?' He started to sit up, then lay back again, his crooked mouth curling in disbelief. 'You're talking nonsense again,' he scoffed.

'No, I'm not.' Margie stuck to her guns, with difficulty resisting an urge to shake him which she knew could easily result in much more than she was bargaining for. 'I'm not talking nonsense, Justin. I think Marc loves her too.'

'Of course he doesn't. Don't be idiotic. Marc has never entered the picture except as a friend. If Catherine married either of us, it would be me.'

Margie gave up. 'You're very sure of yourself, aren't you?' she remarked wearily. 'Hasn't anyone ever turned you down?'

'Only one who mattered,' he replied enigmatically. Then he gave her a sudden provocative leer which made her long even more to shake him, so she sat on her hands to prevent herself from grasping his shoulders. Seeing this, Justin said softly, 'Be careful, young lady. This *is* a very wild and deserted place.' He leaned up on one elbow, his face very close to hers.

Margie could feel his spicy breath on her cheek, and although his closeness set all her nerves jangling, there was a calculating look in his eyes now that almost made her afraid. Not that she would give him the satisfaction of showing it.

'You terrify me,' she jeered.

'Do I? That's a start.'

'Start of what?' she asked without thinking.

'Shall I show you?' Very lightly, his fingers began to trace a pattern down her thigh.

'No,' she gasped. 'No. You don't have to show me that, Justin. That's just lust.'

'And what's wrong with lust?' he asked silkily.

'It's not—it's not love.'

His fingers stopped teasing abruptly. 'Love?' he repeated. 'Ah, yes. Unfortunately that's a romantic emotion that has always eluded me. No doubt the loss is mine.'

His voice held a harsh sincerity and there was such a depth of weary bitterness in his eyes that for the first time, in spite of her own anguish, she was ready to believe that perhaps Justin did know what it was to suffer, that maybe everything in life had not always gone his way. And he was right. The inability to love was indeed his loss.

Unaware that she was doing it, Margie stretched out a hand to the furrows between his eyes. And Justin, with a groan, caught her wrist and pulled her towards him murmuring, 'Why are we quarrelling, my Marguerite?'

'We're not quarrelling,' she whispered.

Then he was falling back on the blankets and she was falling with him, so that she was lying across his broad chest with her parted lips hovering over his face.

For a moment their eyes met and exchanged the knowledge that had always been between them, unwanted and undeclared, that their coming together was as inevitable and inescapable as the river's rush to the sea. And this time no barrier of age or memory from the distant past was enough to stem the need that had been part of Margie's being for so long that she could scarcely remember a time when it had not been there.

Justin's 'sleeping dogs' had been awakened with a vengeance, and there would be no slumber for either of them now until their hunger had been appeased.

CHAPTER SEVEN

SLOWLY and inexorably, Justin's hand moved to the back of Margie's head, tangling in her blonde tresses and pulling her mouth down to his. His other hand still held her wrist, as if she might try to escape, although both of them knew that escape was no longer an option.

When their lips met, there was a moment of stillness, a gentle pause before the storm, and then Justin's arms were around her waist, slowly moving down as his hands explored the body that had waited for him for so long. His fingers pressed into her, rocking her against him, and she made an odd little sound like a small animal at play.

'Marguerite…oh, you're so lovely.' His low voice came out in a husky groan, as he rolled her on to her back and claimed her mouth with a rough passion that made her feel as if the liquid in her veins had melted right into his.

She returned his kiss with all the repressed passion that had waited for release for so many years, as she grasped at his hair and pushed beneath his sweater to feel the taut skin across his back—and the deep male scent of him was more intoxicating than any wine that had ever passed her lips. The coolness of the Highland wind caressing her skin where he had pulled her sweat-shirt up was only a further aphrodisiac.

Now his lips were moving downwards to her neck, wanting to move lower. With a muffled exclamation he sat up, his hand tugging at her waistband. In a moment her jacket had been flung across a rock, and then he was wrenching the sweatshirt over her head. She reached for his sweater, her nails catching in the wool, and soon that too was gone.

Margie had just a few seconds to exult in the dark beauty of his bare skin, in the tough, almost animal virility that she had always known lurked just beneath his smooth exterior, before his body was pressed against hers again, now with nothing between them, and her breasts were straining up against his chest. She could feel his white teeth making tiny bites in her skin and then his mouth found what it was seeking and tugged softly, teasing her and tantalising with a slow, erotic provocation.

She gasped, and when her jeans joined his jacket and sweatshirt she knew that the moment she had been waiting for all her life had almost come.

Now, when all need for restraint had been forgotten, Justin suddenly became very gentle and his fingers moved tenderly, even reverently, over her hips and thighs. When, unable to bear it any longer, she whispered, 'I want you, Justin. Please. Now,' he was still gentle, taking her as if she were a priceless gift, and only giving way to the frenzy that inflamed him when he knew that she too was ready.

Then, when her own frenzy matched his, they came together, and soared together into a wild, rainbow-coloured world that neither of them had ever known before.

And there was no pain. Only pleasure. And a love that for her would be forever.

It was a long time later, when the breeze on her bare skin made her shiver, that she returned to earth, and remembered that for Justin it had not been love that moved him, but a very powerful bodily need.

She couldn't feel him next to her any more, and when she turned to find him she discovered that he had his back to her and was reaching for their clothes.

'Here, you'll catch cold,' he said, beginning to slip her sweatshirt over her head, and then looking doubtfully at the lacy bra which he still held awkwardly in his hand.

Margie laughed. 'Yes, that does go on first,' she teased him gently.

Justin smiled and said he knew it did. But there was a kind of wary accusation in his smile.

'You've had plenty of experience, no doubt,' said Margie drily.

'Enough. But I don't make a habit of deflowering virgins, and I'm sorry. Why didn't you tell me, Marguerite?'

So that was the reason for his withdrawal. 'Would it have made a difference? I know you find it hard to accept, Justin, but in the eyes of God and the law you haven't done anything wrong. In fact I understand the husband is supposed to be the first on these occasions.'

'Mm. And precious seldom is. Do you mean to tell me that all these years... *Why*, Marguerite? A woman as beautiful and passionate as you are... I don't understand.'

The wind grew stronger and clouds began to gather overhead. Margie quickly pulled on her clothes, and Justin, not taking his eyes off her, did the same. As he stood over her, fastening his belt and snapping it into place, he repeated his question.

'Why, Marguerite?'

'Because I...' No. She couldn't tell him the truth—
which was that she had always loved him, and that,
because she couldn't have him, no second best had been
able to fill the void. Her pride would not be able to bear
the look of consternation and guilt she knew she would
see in his eyes if she admitted that. It would be the same
look she had seen that day in Montreal when he'd realised
he was expected to marry her.

'Because I never wanted to,' she stated flatly. It was
as near to the truth as she dared get.

He frowned, obviously baffled. *'Never?'*

'No. Well, once I came close.'

His frown deepened. 'You mean...'

'I mean I was twenty-five years old and still a virgin.
I decided maybe I was missing something I ought to know
about. There was a man I saw sometimes. I liked him—
and he was willing...'

'I'll bet.' Justin lowered himself down beside her and
smashed the flat of his hand with unnecessary force
against the ground.

'Yes. But you see, in the end, I couldn't go through
with it.'

'I'm glad.' He gave a short laugh and stood up again
quickly. 'Though why it should make any difference, I
honestly don't know. As for my being your husband—
is that still in name only, Marguerite?'

'Not any more.'

'No. No, I suppose not.' He stared down at her, his
eyes transmitting a message she couldn't read. It occurred
to her that since the moment they had put their clothes
on he hadn't touched her. Their marriage had been consummated at last, most beautifully—but now it was as
if they were back at the beginning, back to that day when
he had married her and then for almost two years main-

tained a reserved and careful distance. And yet—there was *something* about him now that was different. A sort of angry confusion that she didn't think had been there before.

After a while he put his hands in his pockets and, turning away from her, asked with his eyes on the river, 'Why did you go through with it this time, Marguerite?'

Oh, how desperately she wanted to answer, 'Because I love you, you fool.' But she mustn't. He had become a cold and distant stranger again now that he had satisfied his physical hunger. He even seemed to be regretting the warmth they'd shared. Because it *had* been shared. For a little while they had been as close as two people could be, and there had been a softness about him that was quite new to her. And she had been a very willing partner in their loving. He hadn't had to force her. Vaguely she wondered if he would have tried, and decided he probably wouldn't. In spite of the animality she sometimes sensed beneath his controlled veneer, she knew there was a hard core of integrity in her—husband.

'I went through with it this time because you were wrong when you said I had an unflattering opinion of you,' she answered lightly. 'The fact is, I find you very attractive.' Very attractive! That was the understatement of the year. 'I find you—irresistibly sexy,' she added with a meaningless little smile.

There, that was safe enough. And it was the truth, though not all of it. No doubt her admission would inflate his already considerable ego, but that couldn't be helped. At least now he would be able to marry some other woman, less concerned about love than she was, secure in the knowledge that he had added to the sum total of Marguerite's experience—rather nicely—and without in any way breaking her heart.

Except that it was already broken.

To her surprise, her answer didn't seem to please him. He turned round abruptly, seized her hands and hauled her unceremoniously to her feet, to remark with an unpleasant glint in his eyes that he hoped that in that case he had proved a satisfactory stud.

'Justin! How dare you? And who the hell are you to talk?' Eyes blazing, she swung back her arm to slap him, hard, across his handsome, derisive face.

But he caught her wrist in a grip that was as steely as his voice. 'Don't try it, Marguerite. I assure you, I always hit back.'

'That I have no difficulty in believing,' she snapped at him. 'I've often thought you had no scruples.'

'I haven't.'

As she glared up at him, her blonde hair in disarray and her eyes firing blue spears of ice, she saw something change in his face—and his thumb gradually relaxed its grip and began to massage the inside of her wrist.

'You're right,' he murmured. 'Who the hell *am* I to talk? What are we fighting about, Marguerite? I don't want to fight with you. I want to kiss you.'

Suiting action to words, he bent his head, and the moment his lips touched hers all the resistance went out of Margie, and she surrendered to him as she had every other time he had touched her. And this time the kiss was long and deep and tender, the kiss of two people who knew all there was to know about each other, and yet wanted to know more.

When they drew apart, Justin looked down at her with a wry smile and said softly, 'I'm sorry I offended you, Marguerite, but—while we're on the subject, was it—satisfactory? For you?'

This time she had no difficulty in answering him because now he was not taunting her, he just wanted to know if he had made her happy.

'Yes,' she murmured, eyes gleaming with mischief. 'Very, *very* satisfactory.'

'Good.' He threw back his shoulders and laughed down at her. 'You were pretty satisfactory yourself, my Marguerite. Well worth waiting for.'

'There was a time when you wouldn't have had to wait,' she said quietly, as the first drops of rain fell on her face.

He paused in the act of picking up the blankets and glanced at her sharply. 'No, I suppose strictly speaking I didn't. But I'm not a cradle-snatcher, Marguerite. I don't bed babies.'

Margie opened her mouth to snap at him that she had been anything but a baby, and that the reason he needn't have waited had nothing to do with the rights of a husband, and everything to do with the love of the woman who had been his wife. Still *was* his wife. But she didn't say it. He had chosen to misunderstand, and it was better this way.

'No,' she replied now. 'Of course you're not a cradle-snatcher, Justin. Anyway it doesn't matter, does it? We both know this mustn't happen again.'

She held her breath, waiting for his answer.

It was a long time coming. 'Mustn't it?' he said finally.

'You know it mustn't.'

Dark lashes veiled his eyes and he didn't reply as he continued to gather up the remains of the picnic, and then silently extended his hand to help her up the steep slope.

By the time they reached the top, the rain was coming down hard.

For a moment they stood still, Justin with an arm around her waist, before he suddenly lowered his head to kiss her, very lightly, on the forehead. Then they were in the car and he was driving too fast down the hill.

When they reached the bottom he surprised her by wrenching the wheel violently to the left as, with a screech of tyres, he pulled to a stop beside a rock-strewn field.

'Justin, what...?'

His hand shot out and clamped on the back of her seat, and as she gaped at him, startled, his gunmetal eyes drew her gaze relentlessly up to his face, and when he knew she couldn't look away he said roughly, 'Stay with me, Marguerite. As my wife.'

'I—I can't.'

He closed his eyes, then opened them again quickly. 'Marguerite, I—*need* you. I...'

She couldn't breathe and the whole world seemed to go quiet as she waited for him to go on.

'I *want* you. Don't you understand?'

Margie released her breath on a long, silent sigh. Oh, yes, she understood all right. Justin wanted her. She had known that for some time. But he had also told her that love was an emotion which eluded him. Nothing had changed.

'I can't stay with you, Justin,' she said, the burden of sorrow in her heart so heavy that she could scarcely get the words out. 'It wouldn't work. Today was just— one of those things that happen.'

He turned away from her and for a long time he didn't reply. When he did, it was to agree quite coldly, 'Yes. Of course. Just one of those things that happen.'

Oh, she didn't want to remain in his memory as an afternoon's physical frolic which was better forgotten. But if that was how it had to be...

'I'm sorry,' she said. 'Sorry it happened this way...'

'You're *sorry*.' Justin swung back to her, his grey eyes velvet smoke. 'Marguerite, don't ever be sorry. It was— wonderful. Let's leave it at that, shall we?' When he had begun to speak his voice had shaken with anger, or some emotion very like it, but now he only sounded tired— and the rain continued to beat against the windscreen.

So it had been wonderful for him as well. She was glad of that.

'Yes,' she agreed. 'We'll leave it at that, Justin. And tomorrow I really must go home.'

'No.' She jumped, as he slammed his fist against the wheel and glared at her, all signs of tiredness gone. 'No, Marguerite. You're not going.'

'But——'

'I promised you a holiday, and you're damn well going to have one.'

'Justin, there's no point——'

'Dammit, Marguerite, listen to me.' His face was dark with frustration. 'Dammit, Marguerite, you're staying.' He turned away again, his mouth set in a thin, obdurate line.

He was crazy. The man was crazy. She watched his strong, angry profile outlined against the rainswept window, and suppressed an unexpected rekindling of desire. His knuckles whitened on the wheel and when he bent his head to rest it on his hands, he looked so alone, so vulnerable, that she couldn't bear it. Maybe he *was* unable to love, but that didn't mean he had no feelings.

Hesitantly, she placed her hand on his shoulder.

'Marguerite.' He jerked away from her touch as if it had scorched him, but when he saw her big blue eyes fixed on him with misty-eyed distress, his hand suddenly snaked out and curved round the back of her neck.

'You're not going,' he rapped out. 'That's all there is to it. Stay. Please.'

She knew the 'please' was only a sop to her feelings, and it barely lessened the force of a command which he expected would be obeyed. But because he had at least given the appearance of asking instead of demanding, and because she was too drained, emotionally and physically, to argue with him any longer—and because she wanted to—Margie gave in.

'All right, Justin,' she said quietly, watching the rain on the window. 'All right. I'll stay for a few more days.'

She knew her capitulation was insane and even dangerous. But she had been teetering on the edge of a volcano for days now, and the danger didn't seem important any more.

He nodded, curtly now, as if he had never really acknowledged the possibility that she might not give way to his will. Then, without troubling to answer her, he switched on the engine of the car.

They roared off down the winding road through the stormswept hills as if Justin were hell-bent on destruction, and an hour or so later they drew up in front of the Glenaron.

Margie sat in the chair beside her window with her elbows propped against the sill. Behind her the floor was littered with shoes and various garments which should have found their way to the large chest of drawers, but hadn't. Anna would not have been surprised to learn that Margie felt no interest whatever in clearing a path through her debris.

Three days had passed since she had lain with Justin beside the river, and every waking hour since she had spent reliving, over and over again, those hours which she knew would be all she would ever have of the man she loved. Brief hours, which her memory would guard as a priceless treasure for all of the rest of her life.

As each day passed, it became harder and harder to be near Justin, to watch him being charming to Catherine, friendly to Marc and polite to his father, while he treated *her* with a sort of smouldering resentment that made a mockery of his insistence that she stay.

To add to Margie's confusion, Catherine seemed to have developed a sudden marked partiality for Justin's company, which was odd in view of her avowed lack of interest in him as a husband—and her apparent affection for the elusive Marc.

Several times Justin, still smouldering, had suggested she should tour the countryside with him again, but, feeling this was only courting further grief, she had refused, saying she had been working hard at home and was happy just to wander about on her own when the spirit moved her—exploring the country in the intervals of sunshine, and enjoying the respite from chores.

Marc, too, seemed inclined to take solitary walks on his own, and over the last few days his innate cheerfulness seemed to have suffered a decline.

More and more she wondered what in the world had prompted Justin to insist on her staying, because she found she spent most of her time in her bedroom enjoying anything *but* a respite. With her usual conscientiousness, she had brought her files with her, and although she did not have access to a computer there was no lack of paperwork to be done.

It was the evenings that were the worst, because it was torment to be so close to Justin and yet not be able to touch him or let down her guard for one second for fear of betraying the love that might show in her eyes. Because she didn't want him to know. Ever. The pride which had enabled her to endure the two years they had spent together was the same pride that kept her going now. Justin was always civil to her, despite the simmering eruption that seemed to lurk just below the surface of his politeness, but he gave no real indication that they had ever shared more than a casual friendship. Only occasionally she would see his eyes on her, and behind their cool, appraising façade sometimes she thought she saw a reflection there of a suffering that equalled her own.

Staring blankly through the window now, she noticed a cow chewing with dreamy dedication on some grass, and that everyday country scene brought her promptly down to earth, and made her laugh bitterly at her own naïveté. Justin, suffering! That had to be a figment of her overworked imagination, desperate for some sign that he cared. Which he didn't.

Margie buried her face in her hands. She couldn't stand this much longer. She really *would* have to get away. The only trouble was, every time she made the decision to leave she found she couldn't do it. She couldn't bear to be near Justin, but nor could she bear to be without him.

This was ridiculous. Irritably she moved her arm and banged her elbow against the edge of the sill. She winced and stood up quickly. This brooding by the window was accomplishing nothing—unless you counted bruised elbows. Maybe a good brisk walk would do her good.

As she marched purposefully down the long avenue leading from the hotel, she had no destination in mind beyond that of escape from the agonised turmoil in her mind. Then she saw a figure coming towards her. A tall figure with a rigid, upright bearing.

Damn, she thought. Maurice. That's *all* I need.

Maurice Lamontagne had not for one moment relaxed his deep suspicion of his young first cousin once removed. He spoke to her when he had to, briefly and without warmth, and most of the time he managed to ignore her. Well, he wouldn't be able to ignore her this time. The two of them were set on a collision course.

'Good afternoon,' said Margie as they came abreast. 'Not fishing today, Cousin Maurice?' She smiled sweetly, knowing it would annoy him.

He stopped abruptly. 'No. I'm taking a day off. I believe Catherine is fishing, though. With Justin.' He gave her a smug little smile.

'How nice,' said Margie stoically.

Maurice glared. 'Yes, it *is* nice, young lady.' His white brows jutted out at her like bushy spears. 'In fact if *you* hadn't appeared on the scene to disrupt things, I believe that by now there would have been a divorce under way and a forthcoming engagement between my son and Catherine.'

Margie, goaded, decided she had to fight back.

'For your information, Cousin Maurice,' she snapped at him, 'I didn't "appear on the scene." Your son invited me. To meet my loving family. But don't worry. I'm not likely to get in the way of your plans. I'm sure you'll be delighted to know that, even if Justin hasn't yet proposed to Catherine, he—he doesn't love me either.' Her voice broke on the last words, and she lifted her hand to brush away the tears she knew were coming.

Maurice stared at her, his strong mouth moving slightly, and she thought for a moment that she saw something like—not sympathy, but maybe under-standing in his eyes.

'I see,' he said stiffly. 'I'm sorry if I've upset you, Marguerite, but you must understand—I'm very fond of Catherine. I've known the child almost since she was born and I've always hoped she would marry one of my sons. As Marc insists he's not the marrying kind, of course I assumed it would be Justin. I always did think his marriage to you was the height of juvenile folly.' He smoothed a hand over his chin. 'Not your fault, of course. The blame was entirely his, I realise that, but naturally I don't want anything...' he smiled thinly '...or anyone, to come between my son and Catherine.'

It was the first time he had spoken to her as if she were more than some tiresome kitchen maid who had distracted the heir apparent from his socially acceptable bride. And suddenly it was all too much for Margie.

'Yes,' she gulped. 'Yes, I do understand, of course I do. Please—please excuse me.'

Without waiting for an answer she rushed past him and sped down the avenue as if she were pursued by the devil instead of by one elderly man who was showing not the smallest inclination to come after her.

By the time she reached the place where the Glenaron's big iron gates had once stood, Margie was gasping for breath, so she threw herself down in a patch of tall grass and gazed blindly up at the sky. She couldn't see it for tears.

What was the matter with her? Why was she staying here, putting herself through such torture that even just a hint of kindness from Justin's father could drive her to the brink of hysteria?

She was still lying there, dry-eyed now, searching the clouds for an answer she already knew, when Justin and Catherine drove up, saw her, and squealed to a stop.

'What the hell are you doing?' Justin's eyes, which had darkened with concern when he first saw her, glittered angrily now that he could see she was unharmed.

'Just enjoying the sun,' said Margie airily, scrambling with undignified haste to her feet.

'The hotel provides deckchairs for guests who like sunbathing in the rain,' he replied sarcastically, directing a pointed glance at the storm clouds gathering overhead. 'There's really no need to scare the hell out of passers-by by masquerading as a well-preserved corpse.'

'*Sorry,*' said Margie with equal sarcasm. 'I wasn't aware that you couldn't tell the difference between a live female form and a corpse.'

The light of retaliation flared in his eyes as he took a step towards her, but before he could say anything Catherine had moved in between them and was telling them both to behave.

'There's no harm done,' she said firmly. 'Marguerite is not hurt, Justin, and Marguerite, I'm sure he was just worried about you. He didn't intend to be rude.'

That's what you think, Margie thought sourly. All the same, she couldn't help admiring Catherine's skill at averting what had promised to be a breach of good manners. She would certainly make someone a suitable wife.

'I'm sure you're right,' Margie replied quietly. 'Justin…' She took a deep breath. 'Thank you for being concerned.'

'Hmm.' Justin shot one enigmatic and unflattering look in her direction and told her to get into the car.

It was on the tip of her tongue to say she would rather walk, thank you, but the rain started to fall then, in very large drops, and she decided to swallow her pride.

With noticeably bad grace she climbed into the back seat and had the pleasure of watching the muscular movement of Justin's shoulders and the dark hair clinging to his neck as he drove swiftly up the driveway to draw to a smooth stop beside the heavy front doors.

Oh, dear. Margie groaned inwardly. This evening promised to be an even worse ordeal than the ones that had gone before it.

As it turned out, she was wrong. Justin seemed to have recovered from his bad temper and went out of his way to keep the conversation on a light and impersonal level that included her without making her feel as if she were the centre of some underlying, malevolently threatening storm. Maurice, too, was polite for once, and he even directed a few remarks to her that did not come across as veiled criticism. Marc and Catherine, true to form, made sure the conversational ball kept rolling along whenever it showed signs of bogging down.

It would have taken a very observant eye to detect the signs of a tension stretched almost to breaking-point behind each civilised, calmly smiling face.

After dinner, when the others went for coffee, Margie excused herself, saying she had a headache, and hurried upstairs to her room.

Outside, the rain beat against the windows, adding to the greyness around her heart. The whole atmosphere seemed heavy with gloom and desolation, with some dark, impending doom that none of them would be able to escape.

Half an hour passed, and there was no lightening of either the weather or her own black mood, and eventually Margie realised that, headache or no headache, she must have human company before she became so mired in depression that it would be impossible to pull herself out.

She opened the door to step out into the corridor, but as she turned towards the staircase she saw two familiar figures coming up. Justin and Catherine. Instinctively, and for no logical reason, she pressed herself back into the doorway.

'Justin, *darling*,' she heard Catherine twitter, in an exaggeratedly gushing voice. 'Really, it's been such a *wonderful* day, hasn't it? Just the two of us, out fishing...'

This was accompanied by a long, soulful sigh, and as they came abreast of Margie, still lurking silently in the shadows, Justin suddenly turned to Catherine and murmured, 'Yes, darling, it has.' Then, very deliberately, he put both arms around her waist and pulled her against his chest.

Margie heard a little gasp, and saw Catherine swallow as she gave Justin a very bright, brittle smile and lifted her face to be kissed.

Justin obliged, with great thoroughness and, when he had finished, Catherine immediately pulled away from him, face flushed and glowing, and still with that silly smile plastered on her lips.

'That was wonderful too,' she whispered throatily.

Very quietly, and thankful that she had not been observed, Margie shut the door and leaned back against it. Just as she did so, she thought she heard a third voice in the hallway. She couldn't hear what it was saying, but it seemed to be angry, and then she didn't hear anything except the sound of footsteps fading away down the hall.

She closed her eyes to shut out the vision that wouldn't go away. The vision of Catherine in Justin's arms, being kissed—as she had once been kissed. So much for

Justin's assurances that Catherine was only a friend—
and for Catherine's protestations that Justin would only
be a last resort.

Funny, though, she wasn't angry with Catherine. By
rights she should have been ready to scratch her eyes out
and cast her as the Wicked Bitch of the West. But she
wasn't. It was Justin whose head she would like to see
on a platter. Justin, who had commanded her to stay
with him and who apparently liked more than one
woman in his life.

She ran a hand through her hair, twisting it until it
hurt. No, maybe it wasn't all Justin's fault. Maybe he
had finally taken her at her word and decided to make
a play for a more amenable woman. She supposed, in
a way, she couldn't blame him.

But neither could she stay a moment longer. She must
go now, tonight, without giving anyone a chance to
prevent her. Not only because she had no wish to get in
the way of Justin's courtship of Catherine, if that was
what he really wanted—but because after that scene in
the corridor she didn't think she could bear to see him
again. Besides, he would try to stop her.

Slowly, with a pain in her chest, and limbs heavier
than lead, she heaved her suitcases up on to the bed and
systematically started to repack.

Once, just as she was closing the second case, a knock
sounded on the door, and when she didn't answer,
Justin's voice, gentler and less clipped than usual, called
out, 'Marguerite? Are you all right?'

Her heart jumped into her throat. 'Yes. Yes, my
headache's better, thank you,' she replied shakily. 'I'm
lying down.'

'Good. Sleep well.'

He left then, and she waited until almost midnight, trying desperately not to think about what she was doing or about the man she was leaving, and at last, when all seemed quiet, she picked up her two suitcases and stole to the bottom of the stairs.

The chandelier which hung from the high ceiling was dark now, but dim lights hugging the wall threw eerie shadows across the carpeted floor. It no longer looked warm and cheerful, but more like a pool of blood.

Margie put down her cases and began to move slowly towards the pay phone at the back of the hall. She knew it would be some time before a taxi was likely to arrive, but the reception desk was closed and in the circumstances she had no alternative but to make her call and wait.

The Glenaron's big grandfather clock began to chime the witching hour, and she jumped. At almost the same moment, a tall, shadowy figure rose from a carved wooden chair in front of her like some legendary symbol of the dark, and she stumbled over her own feet and let out a short, choking scream.

'Did I frighten you?' Justin's voice, soft as silk and deadly, cut through the night like the sibilant hiss of a snake. 'If I did, you have only yourself to blame, my dear. Young ladies who sneak around at midnight carrying suitcases are asking for trouble, don't you think?'

CHAPTER EIGHT

JUSTIN'S hands were on Margie's upper arms, and his face, strangely ravaged in the half-light, was bent very close to her own.

'Justin! What are you doing here?' Margie gasped, his nearness and the faint warm smell of whisky on his breath doing intoxicating things to her stomach.

'I went for a walk to clear my head and when I came in I saw two suitcases sneaking down the stairs. Being of a naturally curious disposition, I decided to see who was behind them. However, I believe a much more pertinent question would be "What are you doing here, Marguerite?" I suppose those are your headache?' He gestured at her cases, speaking evenly, without inflexion, but Margie knew that beneath the quiet words were an equally quiet anger.

'I do have a headache and I didn't want to sneak,' she said hotly. 'But it seemed to be the only way. If I'd told you I was going, you might have tried to stop me...'

'And is there some reason why I shouldn't expect you to keep your side of the bargain?'

'Justin, you don't own me. And there was no bargain. Besides, in the circumstances, I don't see why you want me to stay.' As a further thought occurred to her, it was only with difficulty that she managed to keep her voice at a level that wouldn't bring hotel management down on the warpath. 'You said you were clearing your head. Are you drunk, Justin?'

'I am not. I rather wish I were, but unfortunately the two drinks I had several hours ago have not had that happy effect. It's not alcohol I'm trying to drive out, Marguerite, it's something else entirely.'

Yes, thought Margie. It's guilt about me and guilt about Catherine. And you're finding the fact that you're not above that tiresome emotion much more inconvenient than you expected.

Aloud she said, 'I'm relieved to hear it. Now will you please let me pass, Justin? I have a phone call to make.'

'Like hell you have.' His thumbs pressed more firmly into her shoulders.

'Justin, let me go.'

'Give me one reason why I should.'

There was no point now in dissembling. The time was long gone when she might have made a quiet and discreet exit. 'Because I want to leave. I have to go home.'

'What do you mean, you *have* to go home?'

The germ of an idea came to Margie then. 'It's Anna,' she said quickly. 'She needs me.'

'Why?' His voice was hard with disbelief.

'She...' Margie searched desperately for something which would provide a plausible reason for her hasty departure without implying that Anna was on the brink of a premature death. 'She's having a baby,' she finished in a rush.

'Really.' Justin's thumb moved against her neck and began, very softly, to stroke it. 'May I ask when this happy event will take place?'

'Soon,' replied Margie without thinking. 'That's why she needs me.'

'Really,' said Justin again. 'Quite a remarkable achievement, isn't it? A biological breakthrough, in fact. Are you suggesting that the gestation period in humans has now been reduced successfully from nine months down to—what, two?'

'What are you talking about?' Margie eyed him warily, uncomfortably aware of her response to his touch on her skin.

'Pregnancy. I met Anna, remember. She's a large-boned young lady, certainly. But there was nothing remotely expanded about her waistline.'

'Oh.'

'Precisely. So now do you think we can dispense with the lies, Marguerite, and get to the bottom of this unnecessary midnight flit?'

'It's not unnecessary. And I really didn't intend to lie to you. It just seemed...'

'An easy way out? Easier that telling me the truth?'

'Perhaps.' She hesitated. 'What do you think the truth is, Justin?'

'I have no idea. That's what I'm trying to find out. All I know is that I asked you to stay for two weeks, and now I find you sneaking away in the night without even the courtesy of a goodbye.'

'Don't you think we're beyond mere courtesy, Justin?'

'Apparently. So now tell me, without any more evasions, why you're leaving.'

But Margie couldn't do that. Pride wouldn't let her tell him she was leaving because she loved him. Nor could she bear to talk about the scene she had witnessed outside her door. For one thing, it hurt too much. For another, he already knew she had listened to his private conversation with Catherine. She didn't want him to think she made a habit of spying.

'I'm leaving because I must, Justin,' she answered, keeping her voice steady only with monumental self-control. 'You and I aren't meant to be together—and when I go you'll be free to pay court to Catherine.'

'I told you I don't want Catherine,' he said harshly. 'I want you. Apart from which, I thought you said Catherine was in love with my brother.'

'And you didn't believe me. Now I think maybe you were right.'

'And if I'm not? You can't have it both ways, Marguerite.'

'I don't want it both ways. I just want you to be happy. That's all.'

She felt rather than saw him close his eyes in the dimness, and then he said, almost as if the words were wrenched out of his throat, 'It will make me happy if you stay with me, Marguerite.'

'Justin, you don't mean that. You know you don't.'

It was some time before he replied, and all the while his fingers continued to caress her neck. 'I do mean it,' he said at last, in a voice that was hoarse with an emotion she didn't altogether understand. 'Will this prove it to you?'

Suddenly his hands were no longer on her shoulders but wrapped firmly around her waist and, as she stood still, unable to move because all the pent-up hunger in her was coursing through her veins in a paralysing surge of desire, he bent his head. And his lips were on hers, his tongue penetrating her defences as it explored the giving sweetness of her mouth. Because she did give, returning his kiss with all the love that was in her heart, and knowing still, in some deep recess of her mind, that this would be the last kiss she ever shared with Justin.

Then his hands were dropping down, circling her hips and moving further so that his palms pressed her curves against his body. Now she could feel all of him, all of an arousal that matched her own. And, as her arms held him to her, she remembered the riverbank, perceived that in another moment that scene would be repeated, this time in one of the bedrooms of the respectable Glenaron Manor hotel—and, however much she wanted it, she knew that must never happen. Because Justin couldn't love her, any more than he could love Catherine—whom she had only so very recently seen him kiss.

And now, just a few hours later, he was kissing her . . .

With an enormous effort she managed to put her hands against his chest, and when he lifted his head to place his lips in the smooth hollow of her throat, she braced herself and tried to push him away.

At first his superior strength made him oblivious to her struggles, but when it was gradually borne in on him that she wanted to break their embrace, he muttered something which sounded like a curse, and let her go.

'What is it?' he asked, still breathing hard, and with his lips only just parted now, so that she could see the white evenness of his teeth. 'What's the matter, Marguerite?'

'Justin, you know what's the matter.' Margie was also breathless. 'Please let me pass. I still have to call a taxi.'

This time there was no mistaking the words that issued from his mouth, and on some other detached plane of existence she found herself fascinated by the extraordinary range of his vocabulary. But here, now, in this shadowy hotel hallway, she said flatly, 'Stop it, Justin. Be quiet. I need to get to the phone.'

He stopped in mid-sentence, and to her amazement and indignation immediately grabbed her left wrist. 'Don't you tell me to be quiet, little cousin.' His voice held a threatening note, but Margie, her own emotions honed to a fine edge, was in no mood to be intimidated.

'I already have,' she pointed out coldly. 'What's more, it seems to have worked, as you are no longer assaulting my eardrums with the sort of language that would make a hippopotamus blush. And kindly let go of my arm.'

For a moment there was utter silence. No wind, no creaking timbers—not even the ticking of the clock. Then Margie heard Justin let out his breath as, quite gently, he released her wrist and allowed it to fall back against her side. When he spoke, incredibly, there was an unmistakable quiver in his voice. 'Certainly, your ladyship. Your wish is my command—and I apologise for the profanity.' He paused, and she thought she saw his wry smile in the darkness. 'Did you really say hippopotamus? I don't think they do blush, you know.'

'I don't suppose they do.' Margie too smiled weakly, as the highly charged emotions of the last few minutes began to subside and turn into a mind-numbing weariness. 'Justin, please. I really must make that call.'

'Don't go, Marguerite.' He rubbed his thumb softly down her cheek.

'Why not?'

'Because—I want you with me. Don't you know that?'

Yes, she knew that. And if he had said he loved her, then, Catherine or no Catherine, she would have stayed. But he hadn't said that, and without love she knew that he could only break her heart.

'I can't stay, Justin. I don't want you with me, you see. Not any more. Now let me pass.' She voiced the lie as coldly and as crisply as ice cracking on a frozen stream.

Justin was silent for a long time. When he spoke again she couldn't see his face, but all he said was, 'No.'

'What do you mean, no?'

'Just that. I'm not letting you make that call.'

'Justin, you can't stop me. Not for long. You can't keep me a prisoner here forever.'

'I don't intend to.'

'Then...'

'If you insist on leaving, then I'm driving you into Prestwick. Where the hell did you think you were going in a taxi anyway—at this hour of the night?'

'To Aberdeen. I thought I'd find a room...'

'Don't be absurd. You don't even have a plane ticket.'

'I'll get one.'

'You will not. I brought you here, and I'll see that you get back. Now, if you can control your ridiculous urge to charge off into the night like a suicidal owl for just a few more minutes, I'll leave a note for Marc and fetch the car.'

'No, I wouldn't dream of——'

'I'm not asking you to dream.' His voice hardened. 'The dream is over, isn't it? I'm asking you to do something sensible for a change, that's all. Now sit down in that penitentially uncomfortable chair—it will do you good—and wait until I get back.'

Without waiting for her reply, he caught her by the shoulders, swung her round and pressed her gently but firmly into the hard-backed chair.

And Margie found she was too tired, confused and unhappy even to think about arguing any more.

Two and a half hours later, as the car sped down the motorway leading to Glasgow, she would have welcomed an argument. Anything would be better than this cold, crackling silence which threatened to break into an ice-storm at every moment, but never quite did.

It hadn't been too bad until they'd reached the motorway. They hadn't spoken much, but what conversation there was had been restrained and carefully polite, concentrating on the condition of the roads and the likelihood of Margie's catching an early flight. Then, just north of Edinburgh, the left front tyre had blown, and Justin, cursing mightily, had pulled to the edge of the road.

When, his mouth set and grim, he had climbed out to put on the spare, Margie had opened the window and asked if he would like her to help him. She'd said it was only fair, as it was on her behalf that they were on the road in the first place.

Justin had glared at her, as she had suspected he would, his deep-set eyes shooting daggers. 'I've got quite enough to contend with already, thank you,' he said tersely. 'I can do without the powderpuff repairs.'

Margie glared back. 'I'm just as capable of changing a tyre as you are, Superman, and there's no need to patronise me just because you're in a rotten mood.'

'I am not in a rotten mood,' growled Justin, hurling his tool kit violently on to the ground. 'I just don't happen to appreciate beautiful blondes playing mechanic with my family car. *If* you don't mind.'

Margie looked briefly at her suitcase and contemplated smacking it smartly over his overbearing, chauvinistic head. Vaguely she remembered having entertained similar thoughts before. Then she thought better of it. She had enough trouble as it was without the additional one of a body by the side of the road—even a body as temptingly delectable as Justin's.

'I do not *play* at mechanics,' she replied hotly. 'And I fail to see what my hair colour has to do with my ability to change a tyre. However, if you wish to grovel in the roadway without my help, please don't let me stand in your way.'

'I won't,' he muttered, through tightly compressed lips. 'And I am not grovelling in the roadway.'

Oh, yes you are, thought Margie. That's precisely what you're doing, my friend.

She watched with cool detachment as he threw off his jacket and set to work on the wheel.

'You'd better get out,' he snapped. 'I have to jack up the car.'

She knew that he was using the blown tyre as an excuse to hit out at her. All the time they had been driving down the motorway she had had a feeling that the civilised man sitting beside her was nothing but a façade, and that behind the façade was a caveman just waiting to leap out and drag her by the hair.

She didn't speak as she stepped disdainfully to the side of the road. The breeze was lifting the dark hair on his neck, and she gazed moodily at the muscles rippling under his shirt while he worked with silent efficiency on the wheel. A great lump formed in her chest then, and rose up to her throat until it almost choked her. For one mad moment she wondered if his ill humour could be caused by a sense of loss that matched hers. Then she realised it couldn't be. It was just that he was angry because he hadn't got his own way, and a burst tyre in the night had not done much to improve his temper.

Justin slung his tool box back into the boot, wiped his hands on an oily rag that only made them grimier, swore again, shrugged on his jacket and climbed back into the car.

Margie, left standing by the road as other four-wheeled night owls hurtled by, didn't move, but waited with stubborn insistence for him to get out and open her door. After what seemed an endless but unvoiced battle of wills, he threw her a murderous look, climbed out again and jolted the passenger door wide open. Margie returned his look with interest and sank haughtily on to her seat.

It was after that that she would have welcomed an argument, because she could feel the icy barricade that separated her from Justin as an almost physical force between them which remained all the way in to Prestwick.

They had breakfast at a hotel not far from the airport, and by that time pale orange clouds were puffing across the horizon. Margie saw that Justin's appearance was by no means as immaculate as it had been when they left the Glenaron. He had successfully removed the grease from his hands, but there was a tell-tale smear on his white shirt, and his dark blue jacket looked rumpled and as if it had seen better mornings. She also noticed that the ice between the two of them was at last beginning to melt, because there was a look in his eyes now that was anything but freezing. In fact he seemed to smoulder with some emotion she couldn't quite fathom. Funny, that. She had never believed before that eyes could really smoulder. But there was no other way to describe the way that his were burning into hers at this moment.

They ate in silence, and afterwards Justin left her at the hotel while he went to see about her ticket. In a surprisingly short time he was back, with the news that he had succeeded in booking her on an early afternoon flight from Gatwick, via Prestwick, Edmonton and Vancouver.

'What would you like to do now?' he asked her, after imparting this information in clipped and precise detail. 'I presume you're tired, after our action-packed night on the highways. Shall I book you a room so you can sleep it off before I take you to the airport?'

'No,' said Margie quickly. 'No. I—I—could we just go for a walk? Or stay in the lobby and—talk?'

'Talk?' said Justin, raising his eyebrows and leaning over her with one leather-shod foot on the rung of her chair and his hands held loosely on his knee.

'Yes, well, I know our conversation hasn't been very amicable lately...'

'It's been downright hostile,' he corrected her. 'All right. Let's try to make our farewells fond instead of bitter. I'll call a truce if you will.'

'I will,' said Margie fervently—and then remembered the last time she had said those words to him—at a small, quiet ceremony in Montreal.

For a while they walked the streets, not saying much but, in a strange sort of way, in harmony. Then they returned to the hotel and had coffee, and he told her he was sorry he had tried to make her stay when it was obvious that she wanted to leave Scotland.

She said that was all right and talked rather too enthusiastically about all the work she would have to do when she got home. Justin asked her if she had ever thought of expanding, and she said no, not yet, and had he?

'Mm? Possibly.' There was something guarded about the way his eyes appraised her now, and for a moment she wondered what he wasn't telling her.

Then it was time to leave for the airport and the only thought in her mind was that in a very short while she would be saying goodbye to Justin. Forever.

When the time came, it was quite different from the way she had imagined. She had thought he would smile politely, trying to conceal from her that, in spite of the fact that he didn't really want her to go, he was relieved. And she had thought he would shake her hand in cousinly fashion and maybe even bestow a cousinly kiss on her forehead.

But he did none of those things. He didn't smile at all, only stared at her, a long, intense stare that travelled over her with an oddly possessive intimacy. When his gaze reached her face his whole expression froze like a death mask, and if she hadn't known better Margie would have thought he was in pain. Then he stepped towards her, took the small case she was carrying away from her, put it on the ground and, very gently, took her into his arms.

For a second he just held her as she stood motionless, unable to move a muscle. And after that he kissed her, softly, beautifully and with infinite expertise.

At first she didn't respond because her lips would not do what her heart was telling them to, but after a while the curious paralysis wore off and she returned his kiss warmly, tenderly—and for all time.

When he finally let her go, the anguish in his eyes was no longer concealed. But Margie didn't see, because with her head bowed she was running her fingers blindly over his face and down his chest. Then she turned, picked up her case, and hurried through the barrier without once looking back.

She found her seat, between a woman who seemed to be all garrulous open mouth and a man who, buried behind his paper, appeared to have no mouth at all. She sat back, fixed a smile on her face, and adopted the pleasantly vague attitude she often produced on planes when she wanted to appear friendly without actually having to listen to what anyone said. In this case she didn't hear a word of The Mouth's litany of her family's astrological signs, illnesses, weddings and divorces and what Pearl had said to Ruby on the occasion of the latter's annexation of the former's husband.

The Mouth, on the other hand, didn't see the quiet tears brimming from Margie's luminous blue eyes to trail thin, shining paths down her cheeks.

CHAPTER NINE

'ANNA! What are you doing here?' Margie stumbled off the bus from the Schwartz Bay ferry terminal and almost knocked her friend over.

'Your—husband phoned. He said you were taking the ferry over from Vancouver, so I've been meeting every bus that's come in.'

'Justin phoned?' repeated Margie, ignoring Anna's sacrifice of time. 'How strange.'

'I don't think so. He said you might need some help, and judging from the look on your face I'd say he's right.'

'What look?'

'Well, you've been crying, haven't you? And to think I used to believe you never did.'

'I don't,' said Margie, surreptitiously wiping a tissue across her cheeks. 'But thanks for coming, Anna. It *is* good to see you.'

'That's better,' said Anna. 'I was hoping for *some* sort of appreciation for the fact that I've spent a perfectly good summer evening kicking my heels in the bus depot—which is not one of Victoria's more scenic attractions.'

'Of course I appreciate it. I can't think of a single face I'd rather see than yours.'

'Very flattering,' murmured Anna, 'but it's also an out-and-out lie, isn't it? What happened between you and Justin, Margie? I gather things didn't work out.'

152

She bent down as she spoke, picked up the larger of the two cases and began to make her way to the car park.

'They did in one way,' said Margie gloomily. 'Our marriage has been consummated at last—much too late.'

Anna dropped the case heavily on to her foot. 'Ouch,' she exclaimed. 'Margie! But that's wonderful. Only—if it's true, what on earth are you doing back here with a face like a leaky tap?'

In spite of herself Margie giggled. 'You're a tonic, Anna. Do I really look as bad as that?'

'Mm. You do. What happened, Margie?' She unlocked her car and threw both cases into the back. 'Did the barracuda strike again?'

'Not really. He finally noticed that I'm all grown up and I suppose he decided he'd missed something. And I have to admit I was a more than co-operative partner. But he doesn't really love me. There's a girl called Catherine, and I think he's going to marry her.'

'Bastard as well as barracuda,' muttered Anna, starting up the car and speeding off as Margie fastened her seatbelt.

'Not really,' said Margie again. 'Just a man who knows what he wants.'

'Which is?'

'A family, marriage to a willing woman and, from the way he reacted when he found out I wasn't going to be that woman—maybe me on the side.'

'Sounds a perfect arrangement—for him.'

'I know. That's why I had to come home.'

'Did you tell him that?'

'Not exactly.'

Anna noticed the evasive fall in her friend's muttered reply. 'What do you mean, Margie? What *did* you tell him?' She turned the corner into Wrenfold Street.

'Well—um—actually—I told him you were pregnant.'

'You what?' Anna swung the wheel so sharply that she almost hit the kerb as they pulled up in front of their house.

'I—ah—told him you were having a baby very soon,' repeated Margie in a small voice.

Anna rested her hands on the wheel and looked her housemate straight in the eye. 'Margie Lamont, have you gone mad or have I? Because the last time I checked the mirror I was definitely not pregnant and as far as I know that situation hasn't changed at all radically since this morning.'

Morgan smiled weakly. 'Neither of us has gone mad. It was just the first thing I thought of. But Justin didn't believe it either.'

'At least the man has *some* powers of observation,' remarked Anna. 'And I'm not at all sure that I appreciate my "pregnancy" being the first thing you thought of. You must have a very low opinion of my ability to think ahead.'

'Don't be an idiot. After all, I couldn't tell him *I* was pregnant, could I?'

'You certainly could if you were. You aren't, are you?'

'No, of course not,' said Margie indignantly.

'Good. And now that we've established that neither of us is either crazy or pregnant, maybe we can get you and your baggage inside before——' She opened the car door and stopped abruptly. 'Too late. I was going to say before Mrs Fazackerley notices you're back and decides we should be treated to a double dose of veg. But if I'm not mistaken, I see small orange missiles on their way over the fence right now.'

'Undersized carrots,' surmised Margie. 'The kind that are impossible to peel. How is Mrs F. these days?'

'Same as usual. She woke me up yesterday morning by hosing down my bedroom window. I suppose she decided it needed cleaning. Or that I did.'

'That *you* did?'

'The window was open,' explained Anna shortly.

'Oh, dear. I suppose we really will have to do something about her, won't we?' Margie sighed.

'I have,' replied Anna, as she unlocked the door to the house and urged Margie inside. 'I'm going to get married.'

'Anna! You are? You mean you've set a date?'

'Mm. October. The end of the vegetable season—unfortunately.'

Margie laughed outright for what seemed like the first time in weeks. 'Oh, Anna, I am happy for you. But I will miss you too,' she added regretfully.

'I told you you ought to find a man of your own. And *not* the barracuda,' she insisted, as Margie opened her mouth to disagree.

'No. I can't do that. It's impossible.'

'You're impossible,' scoffed Anna. But she didn't press the point because her friend's face had suddenly gone very pale and still.

Later that night though, as Margie lay on her bed above the scattered contents of two open suitcases, she thought that Anna was very probably right. She *was* impossible. She had gone with Justin to Scotland when she was quite old enough to know better, she had invented an improbable pregnancy for her friend, and now here she was, staring at the ceiling and making the quite unjustifiable assumption that her life was over.

Well, she had been through this once before, hadn't she, when Justin had left her the first time? And her life *hadn't* been over. She had gone on to create a very successful business, she had made good friends, and she had bought a house. True, there had been times when it had all seemed pointless. But she had survived—and damn it, she was going to survive again.

At the back of her mind though was the notion that this time it would be even harder. She was a mature woman now—and things had happened that could never be forgotten.

Yes, well, difficult or not, she was going to make the best she could of this situation—of losing Justin for the second time in her life. Anyway, she had no choice, had she? She moved her head restlessly on the pillow and somehow the white ceiling began to reflect a vision of his strikingly handsome face. It had been thoughtful of him to phone up Anna...

Resolutely Margie closed her eyes, but in spite of the jet lag sleep did not come easily. She kept seeing a riverbank, and Justin in a wheat-coloured sweater, and then Justin without the sweater...

From beneath her tightly closed eyelids two silvery tears slipped out.

The next morning she awoke with a streaked and blotchy face—and with another week of holidays before her. Of course she could go back to work if she wanted to, and later on she *would* phone Michael to see how things were going. But she didn't really feel like working. She had hired Michael because he was capable and competent, and there was really no reason for her to put in an appearance today. No, what she needed was a change. Not a holiday. She had just had one of those, and it had been an unmitigated disaster. She needed a change in the direction of her thoughts. In fact a whole new personality would be more than welcome this morning.

Gradually an idea came to her. Maybe she couldn't change her thoughts or her personality—to that of a happy, light-hearted woman who didn't happen to be in love with Justin—but she could change her appearance without too much trouble. Maybe that would affect her mood as well. In any case it couldn't depress it any further because she had hit rock bottom already.

Four hours later Margie emerged from the hairdresser's. Then she decided to pay a brief visit to her office after all. Her reception there was not quite what she expected. Neither was the reaction of Mrs Yamamoto at the corner shop. Mrs Fazackerley, to her surprise and delight, failed to recognise her entirely, but by the time Anna came home in the evening, she had begun to think she had committed the mistake of the century. To make things worse, Anna had brought Bill with her.

'Help!' he exclaimed, coming to a stunned stop in the kitchen doorway. 'Anna, what has Scotland done to our beautiful blonde? Remind me to say no if you should ever think of going over there.'

'Shut up, Bill,' said Anna with unloverlike brusqueness. 'I think it—er—looks very nice, Margie.'

But Margie could see from the horrified expression in her eyes that her loyal friend was having even more difficulty than Bill in coping with the owner of a computer software company who had bouffant black hair with auburn streaks, and who was wearing a bright orange jumpsuit which was engaged in a major clash of wills with her skin.

'Is it that bad?' she asked glumly. 'I was trying to change my personality and my image.'

'Whatever for? Your personality is fine as it is and the tiger image really isn't you. But never mind. You can always take off the jumpsuit——'

'Great idea,' interrupted Bill.

'Shut up,' said Anna again. 'And I expect your hair will learn to lie down a bit once you sleep on it.'

'Thanks,' said Margie, even more glumly.

But Anna was right. In the morning her hair made a neat, colourful cap around her head, and teamed with a pale yellow sweater and trousers it looked unusual, but quite presentable.

Margie made up her mind to return to work.

A week later she was seated at a terminal staring thoughtfully at the screen when Michael wandered in and said that he had heard a rumour.

'What rumour?' asked Margie without much interest.

'That that relation of yours—the one you went to Scotland with—is starting a branch of his business in Victoria. Is it true?'

Margie swung round so quickly that her precariously balanced glasses dropped to the end of her nose and would have wound up on the floor if Michael hadn't caught them in a nose dive.

'Thanks,' she said automatically, taking them from him. '*What* did you say about Justin?'

'Yes, that's the fellow. Justin Lamontagne. I heard over lunch with a friend in the stocks and bonds line that he's starting a . . .'

'Branch in Victoria,' finished Margie slowly. 'I suppose it could be true. He was involved in some business deals while he was out here, but I'd no idea . . .' She remembered the faintly guarded look she had seen in his eyes at Prestwick. Yes, it was possible that he had plans he hadn't told her about. He was very persistent when he wanted his own way and she was fairly sure he still wanted her—at least as a tasty side-dish.

She closed her eyes. This was all she needed. It was bad enough spending every day trying to fight down the sense of loss, the loneliness, and the knowledge that she might never see Justin again. But it would be infinitely worse living with the knowledge that Justin and perhaps a new wife were in Victoria, and that she might run into them at any moment.

But maybe it wasn't as bad as that.

'I expect he'll be putting in a branch manager then, will he?' she asked Michael now, in a voice that was so out of breath that Michael stared at her in surprise.

'I don't know. My friend didn't say. But I guess you could be right.'

By the time another two weeks had passed, and Michael had reported that Lamontagne's would be in business shortly with some man from Montreal in charge, Margie had begun to feel quite safe. Justin wasn't really from Montreal, he was from England, and no one would be likely to refer to a scion of the House of Lamontagne, particularly a scion like Justin, as just 'some man'. No, there was no danger now that she would round a corner one chilly afternoon and run into him and Catherine admiring clothing or watches in the window of one of Victoria's many expensive boutiques.

But in that she was only partially right. It was not in the least chilly, and there was no sign of Catherine as she walked briskly up Government Street the following day, but there was no possible doubt that the man frowning into the small jewellery shop window was Justin.

Instinctively Margie drew back. He was staring at a solitary diamond ring in a blue velvet case in the centre of the window, and she knew that he hadn't seen her.

She swallowed. Justin was here, so close that she had only to reach out and she would touch him. She lifted her hand, and he turned slightly. His cool grey eyes flicked quickly in her direction and then he looked away, still frowning, and with the expression on his face quite unchanged.

Margie stifled a gasp. He had looked straight at her and ignored her! How could he? In Scotland, those last few hours, he had been kind and caring. His goodbye kiss had been one of tender affection. But now, back on her own home territory, it was as if she had never existed.

The sound she had been trying not to make came out in an odd little moan, and turning away from him she rushed blindly back the way she had come.

Hours later, her face whiter than chalk against her newly darkened hair, she returned home, and Anna, after one look at her agonised blue eyes, poured out a stiff brandy and ordered a strangely passive Margie into bed.

By the following evening, the effects of a good night's sleep brought on by the brandy, and a day at work during which she forced herself to be frantically busy, had done a lot to dispel Margie's apathy. Instead she became unnaturally restless, and when Anna caught sight of a familiar pile of vegetation on the lawn she immediately suggested that if her friend was going to behave like an agitated cricket she might as well make herself useful by picking it up as she, Anna, was just on her way out.

Margie needed no second urging, and when, a few minutes later, a shiny new BMW pulled up outside the house, its driver was confronted by a vision of pink shorts on top of shapely legs which were kneeling on the grass while their owner collected an untidy mess of dark green leaves into a plastic tub.

'Good evening,' murmured the new arrival, passing a hand over his mouth to cover a smile. 'What is this? The latest in lawn care, a new style in recreational gardening—or are you just improving the neighbours' view?'

Margie gasped and the neat, pink-shorts-clad bottom immediately disappeared as she uncurled her long legs to rise unsteadily on to her feet.

The man in the BMW took one look at her tiger-striped hair, scowled, and dropped his hand heavily against his thigh as the smile he had been attempting to conceal was effectively wiped from his face.

CHAPTER TEN

'WHAT the *hell* do you think you've been doing to yourself?' Justin's voice voice slashed at Margie like a blast of wind-driven rain, and at once it had the effect of restoring her shattered equilibrium. For a moment, when she had first heard those crisp, achingly familiar tones, her legs had felt like damp cotton wool, and she had not been at all sure she would even be able to stand up. Now they felt quite strong again, bolstered by indignation.

'If that's your idea of a polite way to greet an old wife, I don't think much of it,' she snapped.

'It wasn't meant to be polite,' he snapped back. And then, in a slightly less caustic tone, 'It wasn't what I intended to say either.'

'Really? And what *did* you intend to say, may I ask?' Margie was regretting the pink shorts, which she felt put her at a disadvantage when trying to play the glacial *grande dame* to an expensive and forbidding-looking Justin. Not that she wanted to be glacial. She wanted to throw her arms around his neck, but the tone of his voice and the circumstances made that out of the question.

Justin smiled, although his eyes didn't. 'I rather think I meant to say something like, "Hello, Marguerite. How are you?" But that abominable jungle-girl hair put the words right out of my mind.'

'Don't you like it?' she asked, trying to sound as if she couldn't believe that anyone with taste could possibly take exception to her hair.

'Of course. It's charming. The answer to the prayers of any man who has ever dreamed of marrying a tigress.'

'Well, you needn't worry about it, then, need you, as you won't *be* married to me much longer.'

'Won't I?'

Margie looked into the grey eyes fixed intently on hers and felt something in her chest lurch over. 'I—no, of course you won't. Will you?' She couldn't quite prevent the hope from registering on her face.

Justin stared at her without answering for a moment, then he said evenly, 'Do you think we might go inside? I want to talk to you. Provided you can tear yourself away from this fascinating enterprise on the grass.' He waved a disparaging hand at the pile of dark green leaves.

'Swiss chard again,' said Margie, sighing. 'Mrs Fazackerley. Yes, I can leave it. I've got the worst of it anyway.' As she spoke she bent to pick up the plastic tub and led the way into the house, feeling uncomfortably certain that Justin's eyes were fastened firmly on her shorts.

She threw the Swiss chard into the sink with a speed born of long practice. Then she ran water over it and turned back to face Justin.

He was leaning against the door-jamb with his hands in the pockets of his dark trousers, and his legs were crossed at the ankles. His eyes, in spite of their steadiness, held a very faint trace of amusement, and Margie was as conscious as she had always been of his tremendous physical appeal. She was also, to her considerable annoyance, conscious that he was aware of her attraction. Aware and just slightly—what? Hopeful? Well, that was all right. Smug? That definitely was not.

She clasped her hands tightly behind her back. 'What do you want to talk about, Justin?' she asked cautiously.

'Us. Do you suppose we could sit down?'

'Of course.' She waved a hand at the table, dragged out a chair and sat.

Justin studied her thoughtfully then rather deliberately pulled out a chair for himself.

Margie didn't take her eyes off him. He had said he wanted to talk about 'us'. But there could be no 'us' for them, could there? Without being aware of it, she frowned. Then she realised the table was piled high with the remains of her evening omelette which, because Anna was going out, had remained exactly where she had eaten it.

She jumped up and moved the dishes on to the draining-board then sat down again, her colour heightened.

Justin shuddered. 'Your face clashes with your hair,' he remarked disgustedly.

Margie glared at him. 'I dare say it does. And if you just came in to discuss my hairstyle...'

'I didn't. I told you. I want to talk about us.'

The moment had come. She knew perfectly well that she had been trying to put it off because she was afraid that, once they talked, the small kernel of hope in her would dry out and never see the sun. But it was no use putting it off any longer.

She waited for him to speak.

Justin leaned back in the small chair, looking impressive and yet out of place in his well-tailored suit amid the clutter and debris of Margie's kitchen. She watched him, her heart doing strange things somewhere in the region of her intestines. He seemed to be choosing his words carefully.

In the end, though, all he produced was a flat statement, as his eyes held her rigid in her chair.

'Catherine and Marc are getting married.'

Margie closed her eyes as hope surged—and then was swept away again on a wave of cold reality.

'That's nice,' she said tonelessly. 'I'm glad for them.'

'Yes. You were right, of course. Apparently Catherine has been in love with him for years. I think Marc felt the same, but he refused to see it. And then, just recently, things changed and he opened his eyes.'

'I see,' said Margie, in a small, tight voice.

Justin frowned. 'I gather you're not the sort of woman who goes all dewy-eyed over weddings.'

'Should I be?'

He shrugged. 'I suppose not. Only—I was hoping you might consider going dewy-eyed over your own.'

'Mine was a long time ago. And it didn't work.'

'Marguerite...' Justin's fingers tapped rhythmically on the table and he seemed to be having trouble getting the words out. 'Marguerite, that *was* a long time ago. I know I behaved badly then, but I didn't mean to hurt you. Will you give me a chance to make amends?'

His voice was oddly husky, but Margie supposed that must be the result of jet lag. 'We've already been over this, Justin,' she answered bitterly. 'Several times. Just because your hopes of marrying Catherine have been dashed, it doesn't mean we're back to square one. I am *not* going to fall neatly into line and take her place because you happen to have decided you need a wife and family. For goodness' sake, Justin, only yesterday, when you saw me outside the jeweller's shop, you ignored me. Or hadn't you heard about Catherine at that point?'

Suddenly the bitterness was so overwhelming that she couldn't sit still any longer, so she jumped to her feet and began to stir the Swiss chard round and round in the sink.

Behind her she heard Justin utter one short, very expressive word. Then his chair scraped on the floor and she sensed that he was standing behind her.

'Marguerite, what the hell are you talking about?'

She didn't answer, and, after a long pause during which she could feel his breath whispering across her cheek, he said slowly, 'Oh, good lord. That was *you*, wasn't it?'

'You must have known it was.' Her voice came out irritatingly muffled.

'Of course I didn't know, you idiotic woman. Last time I saw you, you were a beautiful blonde. The woman I saw on the street yesterday was a tigress with a revolting black and ginger bowl on her head.' He gave a bark of laughter. 'In fact I remember thinking some very uncomplimentary thoughts about the things some women do to themselves, and thanking my stars that you weren't that sort of birdbrain.'

Margie fumed silently. Here he was, apparently trying to persuade her to stay married to him, and all he could do was make insulting remarks about her hair—not to mention her brain.

'It's not a ginger and black bowl,' she replied distantly, her hands very busy in the sink. 'It's a stylish black cap with auburn streaks.'

'You could have fooled me. As a matter of fact, you did.'

Margie swung round to glare at him. 'Justin...'

In spite of her indignation, her lilting voice still softened the 'J' of his name, and suddenly Justin stopped scowling at her and smiled crookedly.

'I'm sorry,' he said. 'I didn't come here to discuss your hair, my dear—although I promise you we'll get back to it later. I came to ask you to marry me, Marguerite.'

That was the second time he had said it, and now his hand was curled round the nape of her neck, sending wonderful and unwanted sensations down her spine.

'Don't be ridiculous,' she muttered. 'I've already told you I'm not interested in being your second choice.'

Justin swore again, succinctly, as she turned resolutely back to the sink. 'For Pete's sake, Marguerite. You're not and never have been my second choice. You're my only choice.' His voice dropped an octave. '*Will* you marry me, my dear? Please.'

For a moment Margie's heart was floating on air. Then it plummeted again as she realised he still hadn't spoken the words she needed to hear.

'I can't marry you,' she said bleakly.

His arms locked just below her breasts, pulling her back against him. 'Why not?'

'Because...' She searched for words. 'Well, because I'm already married to you, for one thing.'

'Mm. So you are. Does that mean——?'

'No.' said Margie. 'It doesn't.'

There was another very long silence and then she felt his hands tighten on her waist as he whipped her round to face him.

'Don't you love me?' he asked, so harshly that she winced.

'I...' Margie couldn't answer him, but there was a tension and an uncertainty about the way he was looking at her that was quite unbearably appealing.

'Perhaps I'm not explaining myself very well,' he said quietly.

'I think you're explaining yourself exceedingly well— as usual.'

He shook his head. 'No, I'm being about as coherent as a clumsy schoolboy in love for the very first time.

Don't you understand, my dear? I want you to be my wife—*really* my wife—because I love you. I think I have for a very long time. That's why I could never fall in love as other men do.' He paused. 'I should have known it when I found I didn't want to leave Victoria without you. But I didn't. In fact it took that day by the river to make me accept it.'

Margie stared at him, afraid to believe. 'You—you can't mean that, Justin,' she whispered.

'Marguerite, I've done a lot of things in my life that I'm ashamed of, but I've never lied to you.'

She ran her tongue over uncomfortably dry lips. 'No, but—well, what about Catherine?'

Two narrow white lines appeared beside his mouth and his winged black brows drew together. 'For pity's sake, woman.' Cool and collected Justin was shouting, losing his temper. 'How often do I have to tell you? Catherine is not, and never has been, anything more than my friend.'

Inexplicably, and much to her exasperation, she felt her eyes filling up with moisture, and, as he watched her, Justin's face changed. The brilliant, angry glare faded and was replaced by a look of such tenderness that Margie could contain her tears no longer. But when the first two brimmed over and wound their way down her cheeks Justin gave a groan that seemed to be torn from his soul, and as she stood there, wide-eyed and motionless, he stretched out his arms and gathered her against his chest. Then he tilted up her chin and bent his head to kiss her, lovingly, lingeringly on the lips.

Margie, her heart totally removed from her body and soaring somewhere above the clouds, put her arms around his neck and returned his kiss—because there was nothing else she could do.

A long time later, Justin, no longer looking so out of place, because his tie was askew, his jacket half off his shoulders and his hair an unruly dark tangle, put his hands on Margie's shoulders and said softly, 'Your face is wet. We still need to talk, don't we, love?'

'Mm,' murmured Margie.

Justin smiled. 'That sounds hopeful anyway. Come along, then. As I don't propose to continue this promising conversation backed up against your dirty dishes, let's go somewhere we can sit. In comfort.' Still smiling, he put his arm around her waist and led her out to the living-room.

'There,' he said smugly, sinking down on the sofa and pulling her on to his knees. 'That's better.'

'Yes,' agreed Margie, burying her face in his neck. 'Much better. Justin...?'

'Mm-hm?'

She lifted her head to gaze searchingly into his eyes. 'Justin, if you've known you loved me ever since that day by the river—why did you never say so? And why—why did you kiss Catherine the evening before I left? In the corridor outside my room?'

'Oh, dear lord!'

For the first time she could remember, Margie saw utter consternation on Justin's face. 'What's the matter?' she asked, baffled and suspicious.

'I had no idea you'd seen—is *that* why...?'

Margie started to pull away from him. 'It was obvious you'd no idea I'd seen you.' Her soft voice sharpened.

'No. No, that's not what I meant.' He caught her wrists and held them behind her back with one hand while the other gently smoothed the short hair from her face. 'Marguerite—what you saw—that was a carefully stage-managed production.'

She stared at him, frowning. 'Stage-managed? Production?'

'Of course. I'd have told you about it if you'd only given me the chance.'

'I don't understand.'

'No. Why should you?' He laughed ruefully and released her wrists. 'You see, it was only when Marc saw me with Catherine the day we arrived and, like you, jumped to the wrong conclusion, that it began to dawn on him that he didn't want anyone else kissing that particular lady. So Catherine at last began to see signs that it might, after all, be possible to get what she wanted. Or rather, whom she wanted. But she thought he needed a little push, so she asked me to provide it. I wasn't crazy about the idea of deceiving my own brother, but I finally came to the conclusion that I might be doing him a good turn. We knew he was right behind us on the stairs that night.' He made a face. 'In fact that was the closest I've come to having my nose pushed in for quite some time.' He smiled and twisted a lock of Margie's hair around his fingers.

'Oh,' she gasped. 'Justin, do you mean to tell me I went through all that hell just because of some game you were playing with Catherine?'

'If it's any consolation, I've been through seven stages of hell too.'

'Well, I suppose it's some consolation,' said Margie, pursing her lips. 'All the same, it would have served you right if you had got your nose punched. Poor Marc.'

'Poor Marc, my eye. Once things simmered down and Catherine told him the truth, he realised what he should have known all along. Now he's wandering around looking like a besotted puppy, and both of them are grovelling with gratitude to me. Which is as it should be,' he concluded virtuously.

'Egotist.' Margie punched him gently in the chest.

He grinned. 'Aren't I? Have I reason to be?'

'What do you mean?'

'Well,' he drawled, 'I happen to know you have a certain very satisfactory appreciation of my body...' He leered suggestively, 'But you still haven't answered my question.'

'What question?'

The laughter faded from his eyes then and Margie understood that beneath the banter he was deadly serious. 'I asked if you loved me, Marguerite.'

She stared at him. He really *didn't* know. Even now. And she had always thought he was so self-assured...

'Yes, Justin,' she said quietly. 'I love you. I can't remember a time when I didn't.'

Such a blaze of relief lit his face that for an instant Margie felt as if she'd been blinded. Then his arms were around her and her body was pressed back against the cushions as he covered her face, her neck, her eyes, every place his lips could reach, with kisses.

When he finally lifted his head and sat up, there was a look of such love and tenderness in his eyes, and in the way his fingers gently stroked her face, that Margie knew she would remember this moment all her life. The moment when she knew—at last—that Justin was hers. Forever.

'Why didn't you tell me? By the river?' she asked after a while. 'It would have saved us so much grief.'

His eyes were dark with regret as he pulled her up against his chest. 'Pride,' he said harshly. 'Damned, stupid, inexcusable pride.'

'But why——?'

'Because, love, very early in my life I learned not to give myself away. My father insisted that any expression of emotion was unmanly. When I tried to show him affection I was told not to make an exhibition of myself and, consequently, I spent most of my childhood trying to attract his attention in even less acceptable ways.' His eyes gleamed reminiscently. 'I succeeded too, although not in the way I wanted.'

'But surely your mother——'

'Mother was always busy. Entertaining, running local charities.' He smiled ruefully. 'Marc fared better, though. He was naturally good-natured and resilient, whereas I solved my problems by making Father angry and learning not to show what I felt. Except to children. I didn't have to pretend with them, you see. That's where the pride came in.'

'You mean——'

'When you said you wouldn't stay with me—that our loving was "just one of those things that happen", I thought you didn't love me, that I was just a pleasant way to pass an afternoon. And I couldn't take that, Marguerite. I couldn't admit to a woman who liked me but didn't love me that she was *my* whole damned life, because I couldn't bear to give myself away.'

His lips twisted, and Margie reached up to smooth away their hardness. 'Oh, Justin. I've always loved you. But—I have my—my self-respect too. You only said you wanted me—and I'd been hiding my love for so long...'

'Pride!' exclaimed Justin, slapping his hands hard against the seat. 'It seems to be a Lamontagne failing. Truly the deadliest of sins—and it nearly destroyed us both, didn't it? Of course I loved you, sweetheart. If I'd been totally honest with myself, I suppose I would have known that I *almost* loved you the day I married you.

By the time I left, that knowledge was so close to the surface that, rather than acknowledge it, I ran away. Except I didn't think of it as running away, I thought I was doing you a favour.'

Margie ran her fingers gently across his thick eyebrows. 'Please remember not to do me any more favours,' she whispered.

He grinned. 'I'll try.'

'Justin...' Now her fingers were exploring his jawline. 'Justin, why *did* you leave in such a hurry? Was it really because you didn't want to love me?'

He took her hand and held it against his chest. 'Looking back, my darling, yes, I think it probably was. Along with more stupid pride.'

'But why? Why didn't you want to love me, Justin?'

He shifted their locked hands so that they rested against his thigh. 'I'm not sure I can explain,' he began, in that clipped voice she loved so well, 'but, as you said yourself, we'd been married for almost two years, and in all that time I hadn't once tried to...'

'Exercise your rights as a husband?' suggested Margie, her teasing smile belying the old-fashioned phrase.

'Something like that,' he agreed, his mouth curving obliquely. 'But towards the end that wasn't entirely because I hadn't realised you were a woman. The trouble was, I had realised. But I couldn't believe it. As far as I was concerned you were a child, and I was horrified by the blatantly lustful feelings I was beginning to harbour about you—at all sorts of inconvenient moments. Feelings which in other circumstances I'd have celebrated with a stimulating interlude in bed.' He ran his free hand provocatively over her bare legs.

Margie found herself suddenly short of breath. 'Chauvinist,' she muttered. 'In other circumstances the lady might have turned you down.' When his only response was to laugh at her, she added reluctantly, 'All right, so tell me why you *didn't* try to instigate that celebratory romp in my bed?'

'I couldn't. In my eyes you were still a little girl. It would have seemed like betraying your innocence. Betraying myself, too. Then one night I came home late and saw you slipping back into your bedroom. You were wearing a see-through white nightgown and the moon-light on the landing left nothing to my imagination. When I went into my own room I couldn't sleep, and I was under no illusions whatever as to what was keeping me awake. In the end I couldn't stand it. I got up and went in to look at you. You were fast asleep with the sheets pushed down below your waist and your hands tucked under the pillows like a baby. You looked so vulnerable and beguiling and so infinitely desirable that I don't know how I managed to get myself out of the room...'

'If only I had woken up.'

'Yes. Perhaps things might have been different. As it was, I waited until the next day and then suggested to you in a very businesslike fashion that perhaps we might consummate our marriage.'

'You *were* very clinical,' agreed Margie.

'I know. I still felt guilty about suggesting it, and I didn't want to scare you. Of course I'd no idea you loved me even then.' He started to stroke her hair, discovered it ended at the top of her neck and pulled his hand away again. 'But I did a lot of thinking that night,' he continued, 'and I came to the conclusion that you were eighteen, legally my wife—and I wanted you.'

'And I turned you down because you were so cold about it and I couldn't stand your not loving me.'

'Oh, my Marguerite. What a fool I've been. To think of all the years we've missed.' He shook his head. 'If only I'd had the sense to talk to you—as a woman. The woman I knew I couldn't stay in the same house with much longer. Not without doing something which the law takes a very dubious view of.'

'So you left.'

'Yes, I knew I had to get out of Montreal—fast.'

'Which you did,' said Margie sadly. 'That's why I had to leave too. I couldn't bear the thought of your coming back, still not loving me, and having to go through all that agony again.'

'Oh, my darling Marguerite. I didn't know. And, like the idiot I am, I thought *I* was only suffering from a particularly virulent attack of lust.'

'Mm,' murmured Margie, stroking her hand gently down his side. 'I think at that stage I'd have settled quite happily for lust. After you'd gone I kept regretting my refusal. But by then I thought it was too late.'

Justin shook his head reprovingly, and stopped her hand going further. 'You're an—unprincipled little— baggage. Isn't that the correct phrase? And there was I dutifully protecting your virtue...'

'Oh, Justin.' Margie laughed into his face and put both her hands around the back of his neck. 'Where you were concerned, I don't think I ever had any virtue.'

'Baggage,' he repeated gruffly.

After that it was quite some time before Margie finally lifted her lips from his to ask, in a voice which was husky with love as well as a kind of bewilderment, 'Justin— why are you here?'

He held her away from him abruptly, his hands gripping her upper arms and his eyebrows slanting alarmingly. 'I should have thought that was obvious, my love.'

Margie laughed softly. 'No, I mean when we said goodbye at Prestwick—I thought that was the end. What brought you back to me, Justin?'

'Who. Not what.'

'What *are* you talking about?'

'Believe it or not, I'm talking about my father.'

'*Cousin* Maurice?' exclaimed Margie, with a disbelieving edge to her voice.

Justin winced. 'That's right. My curmudgeon of a parent, who tried so hard to mould me to his whims and always wanted everything his own way. Just as I did. But I've gradually come to realise that underneath all that crust was a man who cared about me—in his fashion.' He smiled wryly and settled her more comfortably on his knee. 'You see, I'm very like him in lots of ways. Stubborn, never really taking time to get in touch with my own feelings. When I decided it was time I settled down, I thought of all the women I'd known, and knew that the only one I really wanted was you—the one I'd started with. But even then I didn't have the sense to take things slowly. I just came breezing out here and expected you to fall in with my plans.'

'Yes,' said Margie dreamily. 'You were quite impossibly arrogant. And very sexy.'

Justin grinned. 'I'm glad you appreciate that,' he said with mock severity. 'It's a habit you'd better get into.'

'I think I could. Very easily...'

He removed her hand hastily from a personal exploration. 'Later,' he said firmly.

Margie sighed. 'All right. But I still don't understand. If you knew you wanted me, and then later realised you loved me but wouldn't tell me—what on earth has that got to do with your father? And the fact that you're here?'

'Ah,' said Justin. 'Well, you see, after Catherine and Marc announced their engagement, Father had achieved his ambition. He'd always wanted Catherine to marry one of us and he was delighted that it was to be Marc who, after all, hasn't left the country. He was in a surprisingly beneficent mood that day, and after a couple of congratulatory whiskies, he became quite expansive—and told me that in his opinion you weren't a bad little thing after all and I might do worse.'

'Well, of all the . . .'

'No, wait. When I told him you weren't interested, he said, oh, yes, you were, you were crazy about me and for once I ought to trust his judgement.'

Margie remembered the day she had encountered Maurice on the avenue leading to the Glenaron, and how both of them had given themselves away. She smiled inwardly. Old Cousin Maurice must be a great deal more perceptive than he seemed.

'Yes,' she said. 'He was right. And you believed him?'

'Not really, but I wanted to. So I decided that I had to find out for myself. I also decided that if he turned out to be right I'd probably murder you without notice—for putting me through all those weeks of hell.' He fixed her with a bleakly accusing glare. 'I still may.'

'No, you won't,' said Margie, placing her hand against his heart. 'You put me through hell too, you know. And anyway, as I said before, a little hell now and then won't do you any harm at all.'

'Bitch,' murmured Justin lovingly. 'And I've no doubt you'll see to it, won't you?'

'Naturally,' agreed Margie, looking prim. 'It will do you good.'

Justin rolled his eyes at the ceiling. 'Lord preserve me from women who want to do me good. Mind you, the last one who tried it ended up with a broken nose.'

'I'm petrified,' she scoffed. 'At your hands, I suppose.'

'Unfortunately, no. She was poking that nose where it had no business to be. Through a crack in my bedroom door, as a matter of fact. As I didn't know she was there, I shut it.'

Margie giggled. 'I don't believe you,' she gibed.

'One of these days, my love, you'll learn that doubting my word doesn't pay,' he said threateningly. But the threat was totally belied when he bent forward, kissed the tip of her nose and asked if there was anything in the house to eat.

'I didn't have time for dinner,' he explained, and added beguilingly, 'because I was in such a desperate hurry to see you.'

'What woman could resist a line like that?' Margie laughed and stood up to return to the kitchen.

Then she paused in the doorway to call back over her shoulder, 'How does the prospect of waterlogged Swiss chard strike you, darling?'

'Negatively,' replied Justin.

'That's what I was afraid of.' As her husband wandered into the kitchen behind her and flung his jacket over a chair, Margie added thoughtfully, 'You know I think we really ought to be grateful to Swiss chard.'

Justin put his arms around her and crossed them beneath her breasts. 'I hope you're not going to tell me that there are lots of hungry little boys and girls out there who would *love* to have my Swiss chard.'

'No.' Margie leaned her head back against his shoulder. 'I expect you would be boringly predictable and say I should send it to them.'

'As a matter of fact I'd go one better. My mother wasn't at all amused when Marc and I packed up a brown paper parcel full of grapes—we didn't like grapes for some reason—and took it down to the post office to mail to the starving children. The post office lady wasn't amused either because the grapes were crushed by the time we got there and the counter smelled interesting for weeks. Management took a very dim view.'

'I should think so. You must have been a revolting little boy,' remarked Margie with a kind of admiration.

'I was, but you still haven't given me one good reason why a man about to expire from lack of food should be grateful for drowned green leaves.'

'Well,' said Margie slowly, as Justin's arms tightened around her, 'if it hadn't been for Mrs Fazackerley I wouldn't have been on my way to the store when you came that first time, and if I'd been the one who opened the door to you I'd probably have shut it in your face. Then you'd have pounded on it and I wouldn't have answered, and of course you never would have asked me to dinner . . .'

'All right,' said Justin hastily. 'I'll concede my undying debt to Swiss chard on the condition that you promise never to mention it again. And now can I *please* have something to eat?'

'How about an omelette?' suggested Margie, knowing enough to quit while she was ahead.

'With cheese?'

'If you like.'

'And ham?'

'I think we've got some.'

'How about mushrooms?' Justin did *not* know when to stop pushing his luck.

'Not a chance,' said Margie.

He sighed lugubriously. But when, a few minutes later, she presented him with a large and fluffy cheese omelette filled with succulent chunks of ham, he remarked contentedly that it looked as though life with Marguerite was going to be even better than he expected.

She sat across the table from him thinking much the same thing, and wondering why just watching him eat gave her pleasure. Then, as the last morsel of food vanished from his plate, it occurred to her that although all at last seemed right with her world, there was one crucial point that they had not yet discussed at all.

'Justin,' she said carefully, 'I think we have a problem.'

He grinned complacently. 'What's that, my love? The only problem I can think of is that your housemate may return before I've had a chance to——'

'No, not that,' said Margie quickly. 'It's just that your business is mainly in Montreal—and mine is here.'

'Right,' agreed Justin, draping an arm over the back of his chair. 'No problem. You can sell off yours and move with me to Montreal.'

'*What?*' Margie leaped to her feet with such haste that she almost emptied the remains of his meal into his lap. 'Justin Lamontagne, I have spent years building up my company and if you think I'm going to throw it all over for...'

She stopped because she could see he was laughing at her.

'*Justin,*' she began again, feeling the colour flare up into her face.

He held up both hands, still laughing. 'Whoa. Hold it, Marguerite.'

'And don't talk to me as if I were a horse.'

He raised his eyebrows. 'If you were, it would take a better man than I am to control you. No, don't start again,' he added, as she opened her mouth. 'Marguerite, I don't expect you to sell your company.' His eyes gleamed with feigned innocence. 'But you can't blame me for trying it on for size.'

'That's what you think,' she said, tossing her hair back over her shoulder and discovering it was no longer there. 'Anyway, what do you mean? How can we be married if we're thousands of miles apart? Oh, Justin...' The colour faded rapidly from her face and her blue eyes deepened with concern.

'Don't worry,' he said, rising and moving swiftly to her side. 'I didn't tell you before, because I wasn't sure the deal would work out, but I've taken over Fast and Campbell's...'

'The consultants?'

'That's right. And I'm setting up shop right here in Victoria. So you see we won't be thousands of miles apart after all.'

'Justin!' Margie's face lit up like the sun after a summer storm. 'Is *that* what you were doing when you came out here that week?'

'Among other things. I was also informing you that I'd decided to keep you after all, if you remember. For which incredible piece of arrogance I ought to have been shot at dawn.'

'Mm, you ought,' she agreed, pushing her hands beneath his shirt to smooth them over his back. 'But I'm glad you weren't.'

'So am I.'

They were on their way upstairs by the time another thought occurred to her, and immediately she stopped dead. 'Justin, what about your business in Montreal?'

'I have a very good manager, and I'll be back fairly frequently to keep an eye on things.'

'Oh. So when did you sign the new deal?'

'Yesterday.'

'Oh,' she said again, in a voice that held a trace of accusation.

'Now what's the matter?'

'Nothing. Only—well, if you were here yesterday, why did you wait until today to see me?'

'Ah. I see.' His arm tightened around her waist and his fingers played tantalisingly across her stomach. 'If you really want to know, I decided that if by chance things went the way I hoped they would, I didn't want any remnants of jet lag to interfere with the outcome I had in mind.'

'What outcome?'

'Don't be obtuse, my darling.' He bent his head and whispered into her ear. 'Surely you know that those indecent pink shorts were made with only one thing in mind.'

'What's that?'

'To be removed of course. By me. And preferably at once.'

Margie twisted her head to look up at him, and saw that his crooked smile had become a definite leer.

'Of course.' She grinned. 'How stupid of me. So why are we standing here on the stairs?'

'Why indeed?' With a speed that took her breath away, he put an arm beneath her shoulders and another under her knees, and carried her up the last few steps to the bedroom.

Several hours later Anna returned with Bill to see two plates on the draining-board, a soggy mess of leaves in the sink—and a particularly well-cut jacket slung carelessly over a chair. She grinned broadly and remarked to her fiancé with gleeful satisfaction that it looked as if the two branches of the Lamontagne family had finally had the sense to merge.

Margie sat up in bed, rubbed the sleep from her eyes and gazed tenderly down at the man lying beside her. Justin, sensing she was watching him, drifted up out of a warm, deep sleep and raised his eyelids.

'You look lovely like that,' said Margie. 'All warm and dreamy and only half-awake and with your hair all ruffled and wavy.'

'Do I, now?' He smiled lazily. 'You don't look at all bad yourself—except...' He hesitated, and suddenly the grey eyes were not dreamy at all. 'Except, while we're on the subject of hair, I refuse to live with a woman who looks like a Halloween party reject. Can't you do something about it?'

'Maybe I don't want to,' she teased him.

Justin eyed her sternly. 'There are times,' he said, in the voice of a magistrate meting out judgement, 'when I very much wish you were seven again instead of twenty-nine.' He studied the ceiling thoughtfully. 'On the other hand,' he murmured after a moment, 'twenty-nine isn't so *very* grown up...'

He grinned suddenly and lunged towards her, but Margie pulled away from him and jumped quickly out of bed. 'Don't you dare try it.' She laughed down at him. 'I took judo once, you know.'

'Did you, now?' He laughed back. 'Well, just for the record—so did I.'

Margie pursed her lips. 'Stalemate,' she conceded.

'Don't count on it. I'm still bigger than you are. And that hair has definitely got to go.'

'Then I'd be bald.'

'Charming. It couldn't be worse than your current coiffure in any case.'

'It is pretty awful, isn't it?' she agreed cheerfully. 'Never mind, it won't take long to grow out. Only a few months.'

Justin groaned. 'Can't you dye it back to the original colour?'

'It wouldn't be good for my hair,' replied Margie self-righteously. 'Anyway, considering it's all your fault, you'll just have to put up with it—as a penance.'

'*My* fault.' Justin sat up abruptly, seized her hands and pulled her pink body down beside him. His face was a study in disbelief.

'Certainly.' She ran her hands across the dark mat on his chest. 'If I hadn't wanted to be someone else—someone who didn't love *you*—I would have left my hair the way it was.'

Justin rolled his eyes heavenwards. 'How like a woman. To do something incredibly stupid and promptly lay all the blame on a man.' Then his gaze softened. 'I'm sorry you were unhappy, Marguerite. I never meant you to be.'

'I'm not unhappy any longer,' she whispered, brushing her lips lazily over his. 'In fact, I've never been so happy in my life as I am this morning.'

'Neither have I.'

It was some considerable time later that Justin, cradling her head on his shoulder, said slowly, 'Marguerite...?'

'Hm-hm.' She trailed her fingers languidly through his hair.

'Marguerite—will you marry me? Again?'

Her eyes widened, and she tried to see his face but couldn't because he had turned away from her. 'But we're already married, Justin,' she objected. 'I don't understand...'

'No.' He placed his fingers gently over her lips. 'No, love, that was yesterday's wedding. I want to marry you properly now. This time forever.'

'Oh, Justin. Yes, of course I will. It's a beautiful idea. Because yesterday's wedding is over...'

'Yes,' he said reaching over to the bedside table to pick up a box Margie hadn't noticed before. 'It's over. And this is for all our tomorrows.'

Gently he took her hand and, on the finger where for two years she had once worn his wedding band, he placed a diamond ring.

It was the one in the blue velvet case she had seen him looking at in the jeweller's window the day before.

As it turned out, it was a full six months before Justin had his way, and the two of them renewed their wedding vows, very quietly, in the small church which Margie had attended ever since she'd moved from Montréal.

He had wanted it to be sooner, but Margie insisted that she was not going to be married for all her tomorrows with hair that her bridegroom continued to maintain looked, at best, like a nightmare occasioned by too much candy consumed over Halloween. 'Liberally spiked with cheap booze,' he had added to emphasise his point.

That had done it. Margie had agreed to a ceremony in March, but not one week before. In the meantime, she sold the house on Wrenfold Street and they moved into a large, bright modern bungalow overlooking the stormy Pacific.

The day, when it arrived, was cold, but the sun came out to give its blessing, and to shine on the bride's shimmering honey-coloured dress which once again matched her long hair.

Only Anna and Bill, now happily married, attended the simple service. Maurice, who was delighted that his beloved Catherine had married the son who lived in England, sent a long, congratulatory telegram—and old Henriette sent another, promising to make her first venture out of Quebec the moment that Marguerite produced her first baby.

'She won't have to wait long, will she?' said Justin, the day after the wedding, as he and his young wife sat in the big, airy kitchen of their new home.

Margie smiled and glanced down at the very noticeable bulge beneath the soft pink sweater she was wearing. 'No,' she agreed. 'Only three more months.' She sighed, a little regretfully. 'Maybe one day we'll get things right.'

'What things?' asked Justin, stretching his long legs and tilting his chair against the wall.

'Well, this wedding business. The first time we were married you didn't know you loved me. The second time...' She patted her stomach. 'The second time there were three of us at the altar, which isn't *quite* the way it's meant to be done...'

Justin grinned. 'I'll marry you once a month if you like,' he offered. 'We're bound to hit it right some day. But only on one condition.'

'What's that?' she asked suspiciously.

'That you change your name. I refuse to be married any longer to a woman who looks like Aphrodite and calls herself plain Margie Lamont.'

'Oh,' said Margie, folding her hands demurely on the table. 'And what would you suggest instead?'

'Angelina, Araminta, Athena, Arabella...'

'How about Marguerite?' said Margie quickly, and before he could get started on the 'B's.

'Done,' he agreed triumphantly. 'That's exactly what I had in mind.'

'I thought it might be.'

Justin stood up, pulled her to her feet and held her very tenderly in his arms. 'I love you,' he murmured, rubbing his chin across her hair, 'even though you do drive me crazy.'

'Do I?' she asked, interested.

'Mm. Utterly. There is only one woman on earth I would suffer flat tyres in the night for and follow halfway around the world——'

'Really?' she interrupted dreamily. 'I've always wanted to visit Tibet, or maybe the Sahara or Burma...'

'Don't push your luck,' growled Justin.

When she opened her mouth to suggest Patagonia and the Amazon or Rio, he closed it again with a kiss.

4 FREE

Romances
and 2 Free gifts
-just for you!

*Now you can enjoy all the
heartwarming emotions of true love for FREE!
Discover the uncertainties and the heartbreak, the
emotions and tenderness of the modern relationships
found in Mills & Boon Romances.*

*We'll send you 4 captivating Romances
as a free gift from Mills & Boon,
plus the chance to have 6 Romances delivered to
your door every single month.*

Claim your FREE books and gifts overleaf.

An irresistible offer from Mills & Boon

Here's a personal invitation from Mills & Boon Reader Service, to become a regular reader of romance. To welcome you, we'd like you to have four books, a CUDDLY TEDDY and a special MYSTERY GIFT absolutely FREE.

Then each month you could look forward to receiving 6 more Brand New Romances, delivered to your door, post and packing free! Plus our Free newsletter featuring author news, competitions and special offers.

This invitation comes with no strings attached. You can cancel or suspend your subscription at any time, and still keep your free books and gifts.

Its so easy. Send no money now. Simply fill in the coupon below and post it to - **Mills & Boon Reader Service, FREEPOST, PO Box 236, Croydon, Surrey CR9 9EL**

- - - - - - - - - NO STAMP REQUIRED - - - - - - - - -

Free Books Coupon

YES! Please rush me my 4 Free Romances and 2 Free Gifts! Please also reserve me a Reader Service Subscription. If I decide to subscribe I can look forward to receiving 6 brand new Romances each month for just £8.70 delivered direct to my door, post and packing is free. If I choose not to subscribe I shall write to you within 10 days - I can keep the books and gifts whatever I decide. I can cancel or suspend my subscription at any time. I am over 18.

Name Mrs/Miss/Ms/Mr _____ EP87R

Address _____

_____ Postcode _____

Signature _____

Mills & Boon

Accept 4 Free Romances and 2 Free gifts

• FROM MILLS & BOON •

An irresistible invitation from Mills & Boon Reader Service. Please accept our offer of 4 free romances, a CUDDLY TEDDY and a special MYSTERY GIFT... Then, if you choose, go on to enjoy 6 more exciting Romances every month for just £1.45 each postage and packaging free. Plus our FREE newsletter with author news, competitions and much more.

**Send the coupon below at once to:
Reader Service, FREEPOST, P.O. Box 236, Croydon, Surrey CR9 9EL**

✂ — — — — — NO STAMP NEEDED — — — —

YES! Please rush me my 4 Free Romances and 2 FREE Gifts! Please also reserve me a Reader Service Subscription so I can look forward to receiving 6 Brand New Romances each month for just £8.70, post and packing free. If I choose not to subscribe I shall write to you within 10 days. I understand I can keep the free books and gifts whatever I decide. I can cancel or suspend my subscription at any time. I am over 18 years of age.

Name Mr/Mrs/Miss ————————————————————— EP86R

Address ——————————————————————————————

————————————————————————————————————

————————————————————— Postcode ——————————

Signature ————————————————————————————

Mills & Boon

Next month's romances

Each month, you can choose from a world of variety in romance with Mills & Boon. These are the new titles to look out for next month.

THE STEFANOS MARRIAGE Helen Bianchin
THE LAND OF MAYBE Sandra Field
THE THREAT OF LOVE Charlotte Lamb
NO REPRIEVE Susan Napier
SOMETHING FROM THE HEART Amanda Browning
MISSISSIPPI MISS Emma Goldrick
RANCHER'S BRIDE Jeanne Allan
A VINTAGE AFFAIR Elizabeth Barnes
JUNGLE LOVER Sally Heywood
ENDLESS SUMMER Angela Wells
INHERIT YOUR LOVE Sally Cook
WILD CHAMPAGNE Kate Kingston
PORTRAIT OF A STRANGER Helena Dawson
NOT HIS PROPERTY Edwina Shore

Available from Boots, Martins, John Menzies, W.H. Smith, Woolworths and other paperback stockists.

Also available from Reader Service, P.O. Box 236, Thornton Road, Croydon, Surrey CR9 3RU.

Readers in South Africa — write to:
Independent Book Services Pty, Postbag X3010, Randburg, 2125, S. Africa.